"Mike, Will You Please Marry Me?"

"Come again?" Surely he couldn't have heard her right.

"Will you marry me?" Sherry started to pace. "I know it sounds crazy, but it's the only way."

"The only way to what? Look, honey—"

"Don't call me honey."

"Why not? You just asked me to marry you. Honey." Now he was pacing. She'd rubbed off on him.

"Because you don't mean it. Besides, I didn't really ask you to marry me."

"You didn't? What did you say? 'Mike, will you marry me?' That sounds like a proposal to me."

"If you'll just calm down and let me explain. Mike, please."

The plea in her voice made him stop. He turned to face her, arms crossed. She couldn't possibly have any explanation that would make sense. Even if the idea of snuggling up every night to Miss Sherry Nyland's sweet curves had him breaking out in "want-to" hives, he couldn't do it, precisely because the idea held so much appeal....

Dear Reader,

Let Silhouette Desire rejuvenate your romantic spirit in May with six new passionate, powerful and provocative love stories.

Our compelling yearlong twelve-book series DYNASTIES: THE BARONES continues with *Where There's Smoke...* (#1507) by Barbara McCauley, in which a fireman as courageous as he is gorgeous saves the life and wins the heart of a Barone heiress. Next, a domineering cowboy clashes with a mysterious woman hiding on his ranch, in *The Gentrys: Cinco* (#1508), the launch title of THE GENTRYS, a new three-book miniseries by Linda Conrad.

A night of passion brings new love to a rancher who lost his family and his leg in a tragic accident in *Cherokee Baby* (#1509) by reader favorite Sheri WhiteFeather. *Sleeping with Beauty* (#1510) by Laura Wright features a sheltered princess who slips past the defenses of a love-shy U.S. Marshal. A dynamic Texan inspires a sperm-bank-bound thirtysomething stranger to try conceiving the old-fashioned way in *The Cowboy's Baby Bargain* (#1511) by Emilie Rose, the latest title in Desire's BABY BANK theme promotion. And in *Her Convenient Millionaire* (#1512) by Gail Dayton, a pretend marriage between a Palm Beach socialite and her millionaire beau turns into real passion.

Why miss even one of these brand-new, red-hot love stories? Get all six and share in the excitement from Silhouette Desire this month.

Enjoy!

Melissa Jeglinski
Senior Editor, Silhouette Desire

Please address questions and book requests to:
Silhouette Reader Service
U.S.: 3010 Walden Ave., P.O. Box 1325, Buffalo, NY 14269
Canadian: P.O. Box 609, Fort Erie, Ont. L2A 5X3

Her Convenient Millionaire

GAIL DAYTON

Silhouette® Desire

Published by Silhouette Books

America's Publisher of Contemporary Romance

SILHOUETTE BOOKS

ISBN 0-373-76512-6

HER CONVENIENT MILLIONAIRE

Books by Gail Dayton

Silhouette Desire

Hide-and-Sheikh #1404
Her Convenient Millionaire #1512

GAIL DAYTON

has been playing make-believe all her life, but didn't start writing the make-believe down until she was about nine years old because it took her that long to learn how to write coherent sentences. She married her college sweetheart shortly after graduation and moved to a small Central Texas town where they lived happily for twenty years. Now transplanted to an even smaller town in the Texas Panhandle, Gail lives with her Prince Charming, their youngest son and Spot the Dalmatian, where they are still working on the "ever after" part. The "happily" they have down.

After a checkered career with intervals spent as a mommy, the entire editorial staff of more than one small-town newspaper, a junior college history instructor and legal assistant in a rural prosecutor's office, she finally got to quit her day job in favor of writing love stories. When she's not writing or reading other people's love stories, she sings alto in her church choir and writes the "gossip" column for the local newspaper.

Gail would love to hear from readers. Write to her at P.O. Box 176, Clarendown, Texas 79226.

To Bob and Celia Young, who always believed I could do anything I could set my mind to, and taught me to believe it too. Thank you, Mama.
Thanks, Daddy.

One

―――

"**H**ey, Big Mike, there's a blonde at the bar." The night bartender at La Jolie shared the information as his boss descended the stairs from the office into the controlled chaos of the club's back area for his midnight "stroll-through." Micah Scott did stand over six feet tall. But more important, he was the boss. Little Mike, the five-foot-six busboy, wasn't.

Micah smiled. "There's always a blonde at the bar, Bruno. Usually more than one. Why should I be interested in this one?"

"Because according to the day shift, she's been here since noon." The slim young man lifted a case of Crown Royal and started back to his post.

"Drunk?" Mike picked up another box and followed. The local rich drank this stuff like water, when they weren't drinking Dom Perignon champagne, and keeping sufficient stock at hand was a continual task.

"Not that I can tell. She's had one glass of white wine since I came on at seven."

Mike stowed the box in the space under the bar and straightened, frowning. "Where is she?"

Bruno pointed. The blonde in question sat alone at the back corner of the U-shaped bar, staring straight ahead as she twirled her glass back and forth by the stem. The inch or so of wine still in the bottom spun and splashed with every motion. Her sunshine-bright hair fell in loose waves past her shoulders, and her girl-next-door beauty appeared to be unenhanced by cosmetics. It probably meant she used stuff far more expensive than that found on department store counters.

"Is she looking for a sugar daddy?" Micah thought it likely, and it left him cold.

Beautiful young women flocked to Palm Beach, Florida, looking for rich men ripe for a middle-age crisis. Or an old-age crisis. Or youthful idiocy. Pick one. Of course, "more money than brains" could describe a good half the population of this town, which made it easier for those with brains to make money off the rest.

But Micah's club thrived because he protected his clientele from the predators. Obvious gold diggers, male or female, were promptly escorted from the premises. Locals looking for that kind of companionship went to the Leopard Lounge at the Chesterfield Hotel or elsewhere. They didn't come to La Jolie.

"I don't know, boss." Bruno looked doubtful as he mixed a champagne cocktail. "Maybe she's looking. Maybe not."

Mike checked the order and started building the next drink, a simple gin and tonic. "Why do you say that?"

Bruno shrugged. "She's not paying attention to anybody here, not making any moves. You know, smiling, flirting, that kind of stuff. She just stares—" He flipped back his hair and looked in the same direction as the woman. "I think she's watching your fish."

The big fish tank on the wall was a trademark of every restaurant Micah had ever owned as he'd bought and sold his way to success. Sometimes he thought he kept buying restaurants just so he'd have a place to keep Bertha, the oversize angelfish that lorded it over the tank. His condo wouldn't hold a tank big enough for her dignity.

"Maybe she's just playing hard to get," Mike said. "Pretending not to notice them so they'll notice her."

"I don't think so." Bruno shrugged again. "Mr. Rossiter offered to buy her a drink and she turned him down."

"Rossiter's married."

"Would that matter? If she was looking for a sugar daddy?"

"Probably not." Mike knew a lot of women who wouldn't care, as long as the guy was willing to spend money—and plenty of it—on them.

"I think she knew him. Rossiter, I mean." Bruno said. "Before tonight. I couldn't exactly hear what they said, but there wasn't any of that 'Hi, I'm Brandy, what's your sign?' kind of stuff."

Mike lifted an eyebrow. "You think she's local?"

"Who knows? I never saw her in here before, but that doesn't mean a lot. She's just taking up space. The place is pretty slow tonight so she's not keeping anybody else out. I guess I just thought you ought to know."

"Sure. Thanks, Bruno. Keep an eye on her. As long as she doesn't cause any trouble, I don't guess there's any reason why she can't keep sitting there making eyes at Bertha."

Mike opened a couple of Mexican beers for some touring Texans, stuck lime wedges in the tops and set them on the waitress's tray before he headed through the arched doorway into the just-closed dining room. Time to tally the day's restaurant take. By the time he finished that, the bar side of his club would be closing, and he'd have that tally to run before he could head home.

He could hire a night manager to do those things, but Micah hadn't made his millions by delegating the jobs he considered important. He'd done everything himself in the early days, before he had any millions. He was used to it. Most days his manager opened up and got things rolling during daylight hours. Micah wrapped things up at closing and deposited the day's receipts himself.

As he worked, he found himself glancing up periodically through his one-way window to see if the blonde was still sitting at her lonely post in the bar. She was still there, always in the same position, not moving except for the back-and-forth spinning of the almost-empty glass. Bruno came twice to offer her a refill or something from the kitchen before it closed. The blonde refused both times, waving him off with a vague smile.

What was she doing here? Why had she been sitting alone in his club for so long? Who was she? What did she want?

Why did he care?

He didn't. Micah shook his head and turned back to his work. He wanted to get out of here at a reasonable time tonight, or as close to reasonable as after 2:00 a.m. could be. He had no business thinking about Miss White Wine out there. Maybe she wasn't looking for a sugar daddy tonight, but tomorrow was always another day.

Sherry Nyland stared into the half-inch of wine left in her glass and tried to force her mind to work. The lack of brain function was not due to alcohol, though they said its effects were magnified when one did not eat. Still, she doubted that two glasses of wine in twelve—she turned her wrist over to look at her watch—thirteen hours now, would be sufficient to do the deed, even if said wine was all she had consumed in those thirteen hours.

No, Sherry was pretty sure her stupor could be entirely blamed on stress and shock. She had to shake it off, get past it some way and decide what to do next. She knew what she had to do.

Find a job, a place to live, a new way to live. Here she was, twenty-four years old, and like most of those she grew up with, she'd done nothing with her life. Her father had encouraged her to follow her friends' example—live the Palm Beach lifestyle—insisting she didn't need a job since she had a trust fund to live on. Insisting she live at home. No wonder she didn't know exactly how to go about living like a normal person. She'd thought she would have more time to figure that part out.

If only her father hadn't come up with his pea-brained idea to restore his fortunes. Sherry had thought the days of selling daughters into marriages as business arrangements had vanished with the robber barons. Or at least with the last world war.

Granted, when she had refused to marry that fish-lipped, pencil-necked creep with the dead eyes, Tug hadn't locked her in her room on bread and water. Instead, after several days of her father's threats, yelling, hissing and pleading, she'd gone to Miami for the weekend and come home to discover the locks changed, the housekeeper refusing to let her in. While she was trying to get in, her car was confiscated with her bags still inside.

She had the clothes she was wearing, and fifty-something dollars in her purse. Good thing she remembered Tug had an account here at La Jolie, and that he hadn't remembered to call until this evening and remove her from the account. Too bad he'd remembered the credit cards.

Maybe if the bartender hadn't come back every five minutes to ask what he could get her, she might have been able to think of a plan. The guy was probably mad because she hadn't spent enough money, but if she bought a drink every time he stopped by, she'd be flat on the floor. She could have eaten, she supposed, but she didn't think she could choke anything down. And she needed her cash for other things.

"Excuse me, miss?"

The deep male voice startled her, so much that she spilled the little left in her glass. Sherry grabbed for the napkins to blot up the mess and found them gently removed from her hands by broad, long-fingered male ones.

"Relax."

If that had been possible, she'd have done it hours ago.

Sherry looked up into a strong male face, its rough planes and angles softened slightly by the smile curving his lips and twinkling in his silver-gray eyes. A lock of brown hair curled over his forehead in boyish fashion. He wore a black blazer over his crisp, white dress shirt. The red-patterned tie around his neck had been loosened and his top button unfastened, exposing the hollow at the base of his throat. Management, undoubtedly.

"Bruno still has cleanup," he said, amusement in his voice. "Let him do his job."

"Bruno?" Sherry blinked at him, trying to assemble her scattered thoughts. *If Tug had to sell me off to somebody, why couldn't it have been to somebody like this?*

No. That thought wouldn't do at all. It could just disassemble itself right now.

He tipped his head toward the bar and Sherry turned to see the young black-haired bartender, the bane of her evening. A less-likely-looking Bruno she couldn't imagine. Bruno grinned and waved. Sherry looked back at the management.

"Can I get you a cab?" He had an almost-dimple in his chin, not deep enough to be an actual cleft, like Michael

Douglas had, but enough to be noticeable and seriously cute.

"A cab?" What was wrong with her? Surely she could do more than just parrot what he'd said. Stress. Had to be stress.

"No." She smiled, triumphant that she managed to come up with a whole word all by herself. "No, thank you, I'm fine." *Ha!* A complete sentence. She was on a roll now.

Sherry frowned down at her empty glass. Could she afford the four bucks for another? She wasn't used to having to keep track.

"Miss." Management touched her shoulder. "We're closing. I'm afraid you're going to have to leave."

Leave? Sherry looked up at him, unable to disguise her sudden panic. At least this time she hadn't repeated the word out loud. What would she do? Where would she go? She should have worked that out in all the hours she'd been sitting here, instead of staring off into space.

She would not go home. That was a given. So, this was Florida. It was May. She wouldn't freeze to death if she slept on the beach. Maybe the solution to her situation would miraculously come to her in a dream.

"Why don't we call you that cab? Bruno—" He looked at the bartender. Bruno nodded and picked up the phone by the register.

"*No.*" Sherry slid off the bar stool, her legs complaining from being in the same position for far too long. She formed her mouth into the nearest approximation of a smile she could manage. "I'm fine. Really. I don't need a cab."

"You're sure?" Management studied her, looking almost as if he might actually be worried about her.

Her smile felt a little more real. "I'm sure."

She picked her purse up off the bar, a beaded satin thing barely big enough for a wallet, keys and lipstick. "I am capable of taking care of myself, you know." She winked at him—it seemed like the thing to do. "I'm a big girl now. All grown-up."

Sherry slung the long satin cord of her purse over her shoulder, leaving the bag to bounce against her hip as she sauntered out of La Jolie as if she hadn't a care in the world.

So maybe that was a lie. But whatever worries she had, she would take care of them herself. From here on out, Sherry was all about Sherry.

She'd spent the first dozen years of her life trying to make her mother love her, and the last dozen-plus years being whatever her father wanted, so he would love her. Look how well *that* had turned out.

She crossed the street to the beach, turning in the direction away from her ex-house. She was through with pleasing others. She was going to do what *she* wanted to do, be the person she wanted to be. Just as soon as she figured out who that person was.

Somebody who could stand on her own feet. She knew that much. She might not know exactly how to go about it, but she wasn't stupid. After all, she'd graduated from the local junior college. A lot of the kids she'd grown up with had quit school after flunking out of whatever institute of higher learning had been bribed to accept them. So maybe an Associate of Arts degree, with no particular major, wasn't the most useful degree in the world, but at the very least it meant she was capable of learning something new on occasion.

She should never have let Tug talk her out of going away to school. She'd been accepted to Brown. But when he claimed to want her nearby, that he would worry if she was so far away, she'd given in. It hadn't made any difference in the attention her father paid her, though, and she'd lost the opportunity.

Sand sifted into her sandals, and Sherry bent to take them

off. She felt a little like Scarlett O'Hara out in the fields
gnawing on raw parsnips or rutabagas or whatever those
things had been. Not hungry enough to touch either a pars-
nip or a rutabaga—not yet, anyway—but just as determined
as Scarlett. She wanted to plant her feet and shake her fist
at the moon and cry out her intent.

Not out loud, of course. Never out loud. She didn't like
to make scenes—that would be a spectacle. Still...

Sherry looked up, hunting for the moon. There, high over
the ocean, lopsided as it neared full. Feeling a little silly,
she squared her stance and raised her hand, sandals dangling.

"As God is my witness," she whispered, "I am never
going back there again."

Okay, so that was vague. But she knew what she meant.
She wasn't going back home, wasn't going back under her
father's thumb. She wasn't going to move in with a friend,
either, and just float through life like so many of her old
friends were doing. She wasn't going to be that person
anymore, the one who twisted herself into pretzels trying
to get someone to love her. If that meant nobody ever did
love her, so be it.

Juliana loved her. Sherry knew that, even though they'd
only lived as sisters since Sherry's mom died. A lot of
people didn't have even one person who loved them. She'd
get by. She had $53.72 in her purse, a college degree and
a sister who loved her. She was rich. Now all she had to
do was find a good place to sleep.

Should he have let her go like that? Mike almost snarled
as he thrust the thought away yet again and tried to focus
on his paperwork. He'd never get done if he couldn't concentrate more than five seconds at a time. But she worried
him, the blonde at the bar.

He should have ignored her protests and called a cab. A

woman alone at this time of night—even in a place as wrapped up with security as Palm Beach—was vulnerable to all kinds of trouble. Especially a woman as out-of-it as that one had seemed. He shouldn't have taken his own hang-ups out on her.

So what if she was beautiful? So what if watching that tiny black purse bounce against her sweet backside as she walked out of the club made him break out in a sweat? That didn't make her a gold digger, did it? Either way, she didn't deserve whatever trouble might be out there waiting.

The fact that every woman he'd been attracted to in the past had always been more interested in his money than in him wasn't this woman's fault. He couldn't start thinking that noticing a woman automatically meant she was after his money, even if it was probably true. That was why he'd moved to Palm Beach. Plenty of guys here had more money than he did. Plenty of them had less, but that just made him middle-of-the-road. He could blend in. Be less noticeable. Avoid pursuit. Sort of.

Finally he finished matching numbers, made out the deposit slip and shoved everything into the bank bag. Not bad for a slow night. Mike went downstairs and double-checked the locks, made sure everything was turned off. He'd taken so long over his numbers that the building was completely empty. Usually he managed to leave with the last of the cleanup crew at the latest. It was all *her* fault.

He should have at least made sure she'd gotten to her car okay. Hell, he should have made sure she had a car outside to drive. She might have walked. Some of the younger set did, especially the tourists, which she could have been for all he knew. Palm Beach wasn't that big. People could walk places. Too late to worry about it now. He was doomed to his guilt.

Mike drove the few blocks to the drive-through at the bank and slid the bag into the heavily reinforced night-deposit slot, then pulled on through to head home. He was beyond tired. Maybe he'd have a chance to sleep a little later than usual tomorrow. If the guilt would let him.

As he turned onto Ocean Boulevard to head down-island to the building where he lived, Mike glanced out across the beach to the sea, hunting the moon path, but the moon had already risen too high. It silvered the white surf horses, but there was no road to the sky for them. He had to laugh at himself, still thinking in terms of childhood stories his mom had told him.

Then he saw the woman walking along the beach, her long blond hair silver-kissed by the moon. Not many people came to the beach this time of morning. Not alone, anyway. He'd heard gossip about couples discovered by the police doing the horizontal rumba after particularly wild parties. So what was this woman doing here?

Residual guilt pushed him into thinking she might be the blonde from the club. Mike slowed down, peering past the shadows under the palms to the moonlit beach where she walked barefoot on the packed sand, her shoes dangling from one hand. It sure looked like the same woman.

Mike checked the street for cops, hoping he could hand the situation over to them and get away clean while still salving the oversize conscience his parents had built into him. No luck. They were probably all handling the spillover from the Peterman party tonight—that was the reason business had been slow. Taking advantage of the absence of police, Mike pulled across the street and parked along the curb facing the wrong way just close enough that he could intercept her easily.

He got out of the car and started across the beach. He was getting sand in his shoes. He really hated that. A conscience was a damn uncomfortable thing to live with. Though he still couldn't see her face clearly in the moonlight, Mike was certain this was the same woman who'd spent the day in his club. He recognized the purse. And the backside it bounced against.

When he got close enough that he didn't have to shout, he spoke. "Excuse me, miss?"

She yelped. Her arms flew up as she whirled to face him, and the sandals she carried came sailing toward him—not as weapons, but as symbols of her surprise. Mike caught one of them and bent to pick the other up, dusting the sand off.

"What is wrong with you?" she demanded, one hand over her heart as if to calm it. "Is this how you entertain yourself? Sneaking up on people and scaring them out of a year's growth? That's twice you've done it to me just tonight."

Mike had to grin. She'd definitely come out of her daze. He could tell he'd scared her, but she wasn't going to let it show, covering her fright with anger. He had to let her believe she'd fooled him. "Didn't you tell me you were all grown-up?"

Her scowl intensified. "Give me my shoes and go away."

"Have you been walking since you left the club?"

"What business is it of yours? Give me my shoes."

He clasped both shoes in one hand, instead. "I want to be sure you're safe. You should have let me call you a cab."

"I wanted to walk." She propped her hands on her hips, obviously exasperated with him. "Are you going to give me my shoes or not?"

Mike looked at her, then he looked at the shoes, then he looked at her again. "I haven't decided yet." He put out his free hand for a handshake. "I'm Micah Scott. It's nice to meet you."

She stared at his hand as if she thought it would bite her,

then gave the rest of him the same look. "Uh-huh. I want my shoes, Mike Scott."

His smile twisting, he pulled his hand back. He didn't blame her for her suspicion, given the hour, the isolation and the fact that he was holding her shoes hostage. "Why don't you let me give you a ride home?"

"What happened to the offer of a cab?"

"I don't have a cell phone to call one."

Her eyebrow lifted in skeptical surprise. "You work in Palm Beach and you don't have a cell phone? What kind of status-hungry yuppie are you?"

He laughed. He couldn't help it. "I *have* a cell phone. I just don't have it with me. I live in Palm Beach. I'm close enough to home, I don't bother to take the phone with me to work." He tipped his head toward his car. "Come on. Let me drive you wherever you're going."

"Thanks, but no thanks. Just give me my shoes and I'll be on my way." She held her hand out, obviously expecting him to put her shoes in it.

He wasn't sure why he didn't. "Why won't you let me give you a ride?"

She gave him an "Are you crazy?" look. "Because I don't know you. For all I know, you could be a serial killer who hides his bodies at the bottom of the lake for the alligators to eat."

"I told you. I'm Mike Scott. I run La Jolie. I'm there every night. Ask anybody. They'll tell you. I'm a good guy. Really." Why was he pushing so hard? He didn't understand it.

"And just who am I supposed to ask?" She threw her arms out to either side, indicating the vast empty beach and silent streets.

Mike pulled out his wallet and opened it up to the pictures. "Look. This is my mom. And these are my nephews." He flipped through the assembly, naming off his sisters' boys. "And this is my niece, Elizabeth. Betsy's the only girl in the bunch, poor thing."

"Even serial killers have families," she said. But he could tell she was softening.

He could also tell she didn't want to. Time to start negotiating. "What's it going to take? What do I have to do to get you to let me take you home?"

"There is absolutely nothing in this world that would persuade me to do that." She held her hand out again, silently demanding her shoes.

"Why? I'm not a serial killer. Honest." He tried on his most innocent expression, hoping it actually looked innocent.

She sighed. "No. I don't think you are. I think you're a very nice man with a very nice family, and I don't have a clue why you're out here bothering me, instead of at home with them."

"I'm not crazy enough to actually live with any of them." Mike shuddered theatrically, hoping to make her smile. Didn't work.

"Why?" she said. "Why are you doing this? Why won't you just give me my shoes and say goodbye?"

"Guilt." That was the only answer he had and he didn't think it was a very good one. And he'd been trying to figure it out longer than she had. "If anything happened to you, while you were wandering around out here by yourself at this hour, I'd feel responsible."

That "You're nuts" look came back again. "You're not responsible. The only person responsible for me is *me*. I can take care of myself."

"Sure." He nodded. "You're right. But everybody, no matter who they are, needs a little help now and then." He knew that from personal experience. "What's it going to hurt to take help when it's offered?"

She stared at him another second, then shook her head. "I give up. Who needs shoes, anyway?"

She turned and started walking down the beach again, away from him. Was he that bad, that she'd rather give up her obviously expensive sandals than get in a car with him?

"Hey, wait." He trotted after her, reaching for her arm, hoping to stop her.

He caught the skinny strap to her purse instead. She jerked away and left the purse dangling from Mike's hands.

"Give me that!" She lunged at him, grabbing for the purse.

Mike backed away, holding it over his head out of her reach. "What's in here that you don't want me to see?"

"Everything." She fought him for it, but the contents spilled out.

"Keys." He picked them up and dropped them into the purse.

"Lipstick." Mike dropped that into the purse.

"Wallet." He opened it and pulled her driver's license from its slot and surrendered the purse to its furious owner. "Miss Sherry Eloise Nyland," he read and made a little bow as he quickly memorized her address. "It's a privilege to meet you."

"The feeling is *not* mutual, you overbearing baboon." Sherry Nyland stuffed the wallet back into her mangled purse, turned on her heel and walked away.

"Wait a minute." Mike had to hurry after her again. "Don't you want your driver's license?"

"Don't need it."

Great. Now she was making him feel really guilty, and as usual, that made him want to blame her. Not logical, but human. "What is wrong with you? I'm just trying to help you out here."

"What is wrong with me?" Sherry spun to face him, anger in every line of her body. "What's wrong with *you?*

I ask you very nicely to give me back my property and leave me alone, but you can't do that, can you? No. Not only do you steal my shoes and you confiscate my driver's license. You grab my purse. And you have the gall to think there's something wrong with *me?* Just go away, okay? Leave me alone."

Put all together like that, his behavior sounded terrible. It was terrible. Awful. Unforgivable. His teenage nephews could behave better than he had. He'd only wanted to help, prodded by the guilt and worry he'd felt after she left the club, but that didn't excuse what he'd done. Nothing did.

"I'm sorry. I didn't mean—" What could he say? His intentions didn't really matter. "Never mind. I'm sorry."

Mike set her shoes carefully on the sand and laid the license on top of them. Then he backed away.

As Sherry Nyland watched him, he backed all the way to his car; but still she didn't move. It wasn't until he got inside the car and closed the door that she came to pick up her belongings. Then she turned to walk farther down the beach. Mike started his car and followed, driving slowly along the curb. When she looked over her shoulder at him, he let the engine idle a minute, allowing her to move ahead, but he wasn't going to let her out of his sight until she got to wherever she was going.

Sherry looked back at him another time or two, then changed direction abruptly, marching across the beach toward him. Mike stopped the car and rolled the window down as he waited for her.

"You're driving on the wrong side of the road," she announced.

"I know." He shrugged. "There's nobody else out here. I figure if somebody does come, I'll stop and pretend I'm parked."

"Why are you doing this?" She held her purse clutched tight in one hand.

"I want to be sure you get safely to where you're going. Then I won't bother you anymore."

"You just being here bothers me." Sherry folded her arms, and glared at him.

Mike just looked back. "I'm sorry about that." But even so, he wasn't going to do anything different.

Finally she sighed. "You're not going to go away, are you." It wasn't a question.

"Nope. Not till I know you're safe somewhere." Was she giving in? He felt a tiny niggle of hope.

With another, bigger sigh she walked around the front of the car and got in beside him. "Fine," she said. "You win. Take me home. See what happens."

He wanted to say something about winning and losing not being the point here, but couldn't figure out how. So he just pulled across the empty lanes of traffic to the proper side of the street. "Where to?"

"I don't even care anymore."

What was that all about?

Mike slid a glance in Sherry's direction as he made a totally illegal U-turn in the middle of the block and headed back toward the north end of the island and the address on her license. It didn't matter. He'd take her home and that would be the end of it. He'd never have to see her again. Unless, of course, she came back to the club.

Two

Mike glanced at his passenger. Something wasn't right here. Sherry sat slumped against the door, all the fight gone out of her. He told himself he was doing the right thing, tried to wall off the guilt that rose when he saw her drooping head, her hands lying limp in her lap instead of clutching that useless purse for all it was worth. She needed to be home.

Letting a pampered local like Sherry Nyland stay alone on the beach all night was as inhumane as turning a crippled parakeet loose in a room full of hungry cats.

He found the address he'd memorized and turned in the drive. "Give me your keys." He held out his hand.

Dully, without any of the spunk or sparkle she'd shown on the beach, Sherry found her keys and dropped them in his hand. Mike walked around and opened the door for her. She didn't move. He had to practically lift her out of the seat, then he walked her up to the wide, plantation-style front porch. He put the key in the lock, but it wouldn't turn.

Puzzled, he looked at the collection of keys again. The other two were definitely car keys. Lexus. Downscale for this town. He tried the house key again. Still wouldn't turn.

"You're sure this is where you live?" He held the key-chain out to her.

She took it but let it slip through her fingers to the porch. "That's what it says on my driver's license, doesn't it?"

Mike frowned and rang the doorbell. It was late, but he didn't care, not anymore. He could hear a faraway echo of sound in the big house, though this one was small by Palm Beach standards. He rang it again, and again. He could keep it up until somebody answered the door. If there was any-one to answer.

"Is anybody home?" he asked.

Sherry shrugged, nothing more. He turned to ring again when the door was opened by a petite Hispanic woman clutching a robe closed at the neck. She stood guard in the narrow opening.

Mike identified himself. "I've brought Miss Nyland home." He tipped his head toward Sherry.

"She doesn't live here no more," the woman said, re-fusing to look anywhere but at Mike.

"Then why does she have this address on her license?" Mike wanted to shove past the woman, push Sherry inside and get away from there, before he did something really dumb; but he stayed on his side of the door. With Sherry. Maybe her family had moved out. "Where are the owners? I want to speak to them."

"They not here." The housekeeper's voice trembled. She looked terrified.

"It's okay, Leora." Sherry finally spoke. "I don't want to get you in trouble. Go on back to bed."

The woman finally looked at Sherry, tears filling her

eyes. "I am sorry, Miss Sherry. It is not right, what they—"

"Don't worry about it, Leora. I'm going now." Sherry backed up a step while Mike stared from the tiny dark woman to the tall blonde, trying to figure out what was going on.

"Wait. I get your things." Leora rushed back into the house, leaving the door ajar.

Sherry slumped against one of the porch columns. Mike stared at her, eyes narrowed. What the hell was this?

"My father threw me out, okay?" she said, all defiance and despair.

"Why? Drugs? Drinking?"

Her laugh was bitter. "That wouldn't be a problem. I could spend my life in a stupor and he wouldn't care. Not that I expect you to believe me, but I don't do drugs or drink much. I've had two glasses of wine in the past fourteen hours."

"I know. So...why?" Mike knew the answer wouldn't make any sense to him. These people—the ones born rich—had their own skewed logic.

"I wouldn't marry Vernon P. Geekly, III."

"Who?"

"That's just what I call him. Vernon Greeley. Money up to here." She indicated a spot two feet above her head. "It's what makes the world go round, you know. Money. Tug's world, anyway."

Sherry sounded like Mike did himself sometimes when he got to talking about people and their relationship to money. Bitter.

"Let me get this straight. Your dad kicked you out of your house, changed the locks, told the help not to let you in, all because you wouldn't marry some guy he picked out?" He wouldn't have believed such a Victorian melodrama if she'd merely told him, but he'd seen it—part of it—himself.

"That's about the sum of it."

Leora reappeared, carrying a small gym bag. "I was afraid to get much. A few things, he won't notice them missing."

Sherry hugged the older woman. "Thanks, Leora. You're the best."

"Your sister, she will be worried for you," Leora said.

"I'll call her when I can. She doesn't need to be in the middle of this. I'll be fine." Sherry smiled with an assurance Mike was pretty sure she didn't feel.

"I only wish I could do more." Leora apologized once more with a look and vanished inside, locking the door again.

Sherry picked up the bag and walked off the porch.

Mike trailed after her. "What are you going to do now?"

"Get a job. Find a place to live."

"No, I mean now. Right now. Tonight."

"It's morning."

"Don't be difficult. Where are you going?"

She shrugged. "I'll figure something out."

Mike took a deep breath. It was stupid…he knew it was stupid…and he was going to do it anyway. "Come on." He took her elbow and steered her back to the car.

"What? Let go of me." Sherry tried to pull away with as much success as could be expected. None. "Isn't humiliating me like this enough for you?"

He shook his head. "I have to be out of my mind." He opened his trunk and tossed her bag in. "Because I'm taking you home with me."

Sherry backed away. "No way. Forget it. I'm not going home with you. Just give me back my bag and I'll get out of your way." She didn't know why he offered, but she wasn't dumb enough to take him up on it. Bad enough she'd let him drive her here.

"Don't be stupid. Where else are you going to go?" He beckoned to her. "Get in the car."

"I'm not going with you." She didn't know anything about him, except that he was as stubborn as the day was long and built like a Greek god. And he had a bunch of cute nephews and a silver-haired mother. And he worked at La Jolie. Management, even. Okay, so maybe she did know a little about him. But it wasn't enough.

"Yes, you are. Now quit arguing and come on." He reached for her.

Sherry skittered out of his way, jerking her arms back. She wasn't about to let him get hold of her. "Your over-grown sense of responsibility again? Give it a rest."

He propped his hands on his hips and stared at the concrete of the drive as he gave a long sigh. "Don't you think I would if I could? Especially when I could be at home sleeping?"

She scowled, suspicious. She hadn't been suspicious enough in her life, and it was past time to start. Besides, she wanted to go with him. Too much. Which had to mean it was a really bad idea. He couldn't possibly be as nice as he seemed. "If I were a guy, you wouldn't be offering to take me home, would you?"

"If you were a guy, you could protect yourself."

"I can protect myself just fine."

"Sure. If I'd wanted to, I could have carried you off the beach instead of just…" He looked embarrassed as he gestured at her purse. "You know."

Sherry felt the heat rise to her face. In the end, he hadn't had to. She'd gone with him willingly. "I would have screamed."

"And nobody would have heard you."

They were getting away from the point Sherry was trying

to make. "Okay, fine. But if I were forty years old and fat, would you still take me home with you?"

"If you had no place else to go, and helpless as you are? Yeah. I would. In fact, I did. Well, it was a couple—husband and wife. They got robbed just outside the club, needed a place to stay long enough to pick up a wire from back home." He glared at her. "You want references?"

"Please." She didn't understand him. His attitude was totally outside her frame of reference.

"Sorry. They're a little hard to come by at this time of night."

"Just tell me why. Make me believe it. *Why* are you doing this?" If she could understand, maybe she could believe him. His offer was a lot more appealing than her other prospects. And the appeal didn't have anything to do with the way his shoulders filled out that suit coat. Much.

He sighed, looking away. He started to speak, hesitated, then tried again, as if the words were too hard to say. "I've been where you are," he said. "In Pensacola, years ago. Broke, stranded, no place to stay because people I trusted—guys I was going into business with—ran off with everything I had. Somebody helped me then. He gave me a place to sleep. Helped me get back on my feet. So I know, okay? I know what it feels like."

Sherry found her suspicions lowering. Probably far more than they should. "I can sleep on the beach," she said, trying one more time.

"No, you can't. It's not safe." He sighed. "Look."

The way his fingers spread on his hips, made her do as he said—look. Exactly where she shouldn't. "It's just for tonight. My mom lives in the apartment next door. I'd take you there if it wasn't so late, but she's…not well. Too sick for me to wake her up in the middle of the night. I'm just offering a bathroom and a place to sleep. Breakfast if you want it. That's all."

She still hesitated. "You're sure?"

"Yes." He sounded tired. "Are you coming? Or do I have to follow you down the street? Again."

"Aren't you getting tired of following me?"

"Yes. Aren't you getting tired of running?"

Sherry took a deep breath and let her eyelids fall closed. "Truthfully, yes. I am." She was tired of so many things.

He opened the passenger side door for her. "Come on," he said. "You can start fresh tomorrow." Then he smiled.

Mike Scott smiling was a sight that should be outlawed, declared a controlled substance. It had too great a possibility of becoming addictive. His eyes crinkled up at the corners, and a dimple appeared in one cheek. Only one, which made it even more appealing.

Sherry got in the car. He started it, a late-model American midsize of some kind—Sherry didn't know much about cars—and headed south again. As he drove, he tapped on the steering wheel in rhythm to some private music.

"What did your mom say when your dad pulled this stunt?" he said.

"I imagine she would have said plenty." Sherry smiled at the thought. "But she died. A long time ago. I was almost twelve. It was a boating accident. My parents were divorced a long time before that, though. When Mom died, I went to live with Tug and Bebe, my dad and stepmother."

"I'm sorry."

"It was a long time ago. But thanks."

"Sure. I know how it is to lose a parent. It's never easy."

"I thought you said your mom—"

"My dad. A couple of years ago."

"Ah."

They rode in silence a moment or two. Until Sherry couldn't stand the silence. "Mr. Scott—"

"Call me Mike." He slanted a glance her direction.

"Mike."

He smiled again, just a little one, but it caused the same reaction in Sherry as his grown-up smiles. Total discombobulation.

"Did you want something?" he asked.

"I forgot." She had no clue what she'd intended to say. The man was bad for her concentration.

"What about brothers or sisters?" Mike said. "Didn't the maid say you have a sister?"

"Half sister. Juliana. She lives there, too. There's just the two of us, besides Tug and Bebe."

"She didn't say anything? How old is she?"

"Almost twenty-two. But she probably doesn't even know what happened. Tug and Bebe don't tell her much. They have this need-to-know policy when it comes to Juliana, to protect her. I do, too, I guess. She's the helpless one." She grinned at Mike. "I, on the other hand, can take care of myself."

Mike smiled, but didn't respond to her teasing. He rocked his head in time to his silent music as they drove across Palm Beach. The city was quiet, businesses and homes dark and sleeping. Sherry fought the weariness that sapped her, but lost the battle in two blocks.

In the parking garage beside his building, Mike wondered if Sherry would wake up, or if he would have to carry her in. He hoped for waking. It was a long way up to the eighth floor, even with elevators. Besides, if he carried her inside and put her in bed, he wasn't sure he had the willpower to keep from crawling in with her. He was already too tempted where she was concerned.

He needed her awake and prickly with defenses in order to keep him in line. She looked too soft and vulnerable, curled up in the other seat. Too much like she could belong there, and that wasn't right. Never would be. He had to keep reminding himself. She was from Palm Beach, home of the money worshippers.

The slam of the trunk had her stirring, opening the car door. Mike hurried forward to catch her arm. Half-asleep and clumsy with it, she could easily fall.

"Are we there yet?" she mumbled.

"Yeah." He smiled, getting an arm around her to hold her upright. Her sleepy confusion was cute as hell, and the feel of her in his arms lowered his resistance further. "We're here."

Mike kicked the car door shut and steered her to the elevator. In the lobby they made the switch to the building elevator and rode it to the top. His apartment was in the corner. He could smell the pot roast the minute he got inside, and he swore.

At the oath, Sherry startled, bashing her head into his jaw.

"Careful." He urged her toward a chair and went through to the kitchen to turn off the stove, swearing again.

"What's wrong?" She yawned, jaw popping.

"Mom left supper cooking, that's what." He grabbed a hot pad and flipped the oven door open. "I told her not to do it. I told her I'd get something before I came home. I work at a restaurant. It's no trouble. She doesn't need to be coming over here, cooking for me. She needs to rest, dammit. She never listens to me."

He set the steaming roaster pan on top of the stove, and his glance fell on Sherry where she'd followed him into the kitchen. She was smiling, as if she knew something he didn't. "What?"

"I wonder how many times your mom has said 'he never listens to me.'"

All his frustration slid away, just looking at her smile.

She was beautiful anytime, but when she smiled, he couldn't find air—and he needed all he could get.

"She probably said it a million times," Mike admitted, trying to keep his mind where it belonged. "I'm pretty hardheaded."

Sherry laughed, and he went dizzy. "That's putting it mildly. You define *stubborn*."

"You're right in there with me, little girl."

"I'm not a little girl. Remember?"

He knew it. Which was the whole problem.

Her stomach growled audibly and he frowned. "Have you had anything to eat today?"

Probably not. Not since noon, he knew for sure. He got a plate out of the cabinet and piled it with meat, potatoes and carrots from the dinner his mom wasn't supposed to cook.

"Here." Mike set the plate in front of her, along with a knife and fork. "Mom makes the best pot roast in the world, and if nobody eats it, her feelings will be hurt. Want a soda to go with that?"

"Thanks. Why aren't you having any, if it's so good?"

Mike set a can of something on the table, got another for himself and sat across from her, thinking he wouldn't be so tempted with the table between them. Now he couldn't avoid looking at her, which was a problem because he liked looking at her way too much.

"I already ate," he said. "Like I told Mom I would."

"Oh." She took a bite, testing the waters, then dove in. "I guess this makes you the favorite son, then."

He watched, spellbound, as her tongue licked gravy off the fork. "I'm the only son."

Talk. If he kept the conversation going, maybe she wouldn't notice his preoccupation. "I've got two older sisters. The ones with all the boys. They don't have time to look after Mom."

He had always thought those scenes in movies where people ate while making eyes at each other were totally stupid. Eating was eating and sex was sex. But watching Sherry Nyland eat was fast changing his mind.

The way her lips closed around the fork as she pulled it from her mouth made him wonder things he had no business wondering. Like if those lips would close and cling the same way to other objects. And when her pink tongue licked out of her mouth across her lip, he wanted to capture it, wanted it licking across his lips. And other places.

"Mike." Sherry said his name as if she'd said it a few times already.

"Yeah. What?" He forced his gaze away from her mouth to her eyes and ordered himself to keep it there.

"Where were you?"

His face went hot, even though it couldn't be. He never blushed. "Nowhere. Right here."

"Could have fooled me." She took another bite of roast, but this time he didn't watch. "I was about ready to try radio signals to outer space."

"Just tired, I guess." Mike tried to look casual, disinterested, tired. Something besides dumb, which was how he probably looked. "It's been a long day."

"Sorry." Her eyelashes made little shadows on her cheeks when she looked down at her plate.

"For what?"

"For making you chase around after me after you got off work."

"Oh, that." He relaxed. He'd been worried for a minute that she was going to try to leave again, or do something else crazy. "Don't worry about it. I didn't mind."

"It was nice. Actually, I do appreciate it," she said. "You didn't have to be so nice to me."

"What was nice? I acted worse than one of my nephews. I grabbed your purse."

Sherry put her fork down and glared at him. "You stop that, this instant. If I say you were nice, then you were nice. Does that ruin your big, bad bartender image? Well, too bad. Because you are a nice man, Michael Scott. And if I want to thank you for being nice to me, you are going to sit there and take it. Okay?" She waved a hand.

"Okay." He had to work to keep a straight face. She was cute when she got all riled up. Like a kitten in a hissing fit. "And it's Micah."

"What?"

"My name. It's not Michael. It's Micah. Like in the Bible. Old family name. Remember? I told you."

"Oh." She seemed disappointed he didn't want to argue. "I guess I didn't hear you."

"You're welcome, by the way." He wanted to take her hand, but he'd promised her nothing but a place to sleep. And he'd promised himself he'd stay away from Palm Beach beauties. Hand-holding wasn't allowed. Nor was holding any of the other things floating through his mind— like her body against his.

"I guess I have a hard time thinking of myself that way. You know. Nice." He drank down the last of his soda. "I just do what needs doing. You about done with that plate?"

Sherry blinked, as if he'd surprised her. "Yes, thank you. It was delicious."

"I'll tell Mom you said so." Mike carried her plate to the dishwasher. "Come on. I'll show you where you can sleep."

"I can take the couch," she said as he led her through the living room to the back of the apartment. "I'll probably fit better than you."

"No need." He opened the door to his office/guest room. "No guarantee on the quality of the mattress. My oldest sister handed it down to me when they got a new bed for her oldest. But it *is* guaranteed to be better than the beach."

"Thanks." She surveyed the room and smiled up at him. "I really do appreciate this."

With her smiling at him like that, Mike had trouble finding his words. "You're welcome."

He beat a hasty retreat. He had to keep his distance, make sure she understood he didn't play her kind of games. He heard her door close a fraction of a second before he closed his. Good.

Sherry woke up from a dream of Mike's thundercloud-gray eyes staring at her, swallowing her up, stripping her bare, right past her skin clear down to her soul. She was so disoriented that, for a minute, she didn't realize the sharp rapping was someone knocking on a door, rather than the pounding of her heart.

Where was Mike? Why wasn't he answering the door?

Sherry scooted out of bed and opened the bedroom door. Immediately she heard distant shower noises. That explained it. She pulled shorts on under her Tweety-bird sleep shirt, ran her hands through her hair so it didn't look quite so wild, and stepped out into the hallway at the exact same moment that a dripping-wet Mike, clad only in a towel, stepped out of the opposite bedroom.

She stood nose to nose with his wet, naked chest. Which, she decided, meant that it was more nose to sternum. Nose to collarbone.

Water had plastered down the faint drift of hair across the center of his chest and followed the trail leading down from his navel to vanish beneath the towel he held clutched at one hip. The towel that gaped open to expose a tanned, muscular thigh and an inch or so of untanned hip. She couldn't help herself. She had to look. He was the most magnificent specimen of human male she'd ever seen.

Just then Mike's front door opened, the door directly across the spacious living room from the hallway where they stood, and a tiny, thin, silver-haired woman danced slowly into the room. She saw Mike and Sherry standing toe-to-toe in the hallway. Her eyes got big and round, and she grinned. Ear to ear.

"Oops." She covered her mouth with a hand, for all the world like a naughty child. "Don't mind me. I'm not here. Forget I ever came in." She turned and headed for the door again.

Mike swore. He started across the living room toward his mother—she could be no one else—then looked down at his state of undress, looked up at Sherry and back at his mother. He swore again, under his breath this time.

"Don't let her leave." He ground the words through his teeth at Sherry as he vanished back into his bedroom.

"Mrs. Scott, wait." Sherry darted across the room to take the woman's arm. It was like handling a songbird, the older woman felt so fragile.

"No, no, I'll go. Don't let me interrupt."

"You weren't interrupting a thing, Mrs. Scott." Sherry steered her back into the room and lowered her into one of the fat, leather club chairs. "Except maybe Mike's shower."

"I wasn't?"

"No, ma'am."

"Well, *darn.*" Mike's mother looked so disappointed that Sherry had to laugh. "I was hoping he'd brought some sweet young thing home for a little fun and frolic."

"I gave up frolicking years ago," Mike said, coming back out of the bedroom, pulling on a baby-blue polo shirt as he did. Sherry held her breath until he got it down over that distracting chest and abdomen.

"You shouldn't have." Mrs. Scott shook her finger at her son. "All work and no frolic makes Micah a dull boy."

"Besides, I'm no sweet young thing," Sherry said. "I'm a homeless vagrant he found in a bar."

The look Mike shot her as he bent to kiss his mother on the cheek sent flames rushing through Sherry, center out, until she burned head to toe.

"You're not supposed to come over here without your oxygen," Mike scolded gently.

"Oh, fiddle. I can walk five feet without sucking on that thing."

"Mom, we made a deal, remember?"

"Aren't you going to introduce me to your friend, the vagrant?" She smiled determinedly at Sherry, ignoring Mike.

He sighed, long and slow. The way he'd sighed at Sherry so often last night. "Mom, this is Sherry Nyland. Sherry, this is my mom."

"It's nice to meet you, Mrs. Scott." Sherry put her hand out to shake, feeling a little peculiar to be making someone's acquaintance while she was dressed for sleeping. This wasn't usually how it was done in Palm Beach. But it was interesting. Part of her adventure.

"Please, call me Clara." Mike's mother took Sherry's hand in a surprisingly strong grip and squeezed once, then used her grip to pull Sherry down into the chair beside hers. "So, what do you think of my handsome son?"

Sherry glanced at Mike, expecting some protest, but he just rolled his eyes and padded away on bare feet, sighing as he went.

"He is handsome," she agreed. "He's nice, too. By the way, you make a terrific pot roast. He gave me some last night."

"Which I told you not to cook." He called from the open kitchen where he was clattering around.

"And what would you have given Sherry to eat if I hadn't?" Clara winked at Sherry and patted her hand.

Mike put his head through the open doorway. "Bologna sandwiches."

"See? Pot roast is much better."

He growled and vanished. Sherry tried to hide her laughter.

Clara didn't. "How did you two meet?"

"At La Jolie. He had to throw me out at closing."

"No, really. How did you meet?"

"I didn't throw you out," Mike said from the kitchen. "I just told you we were closing and suggested it was time to go home."

Sherry nodded, chuckling as Clara's eyes got big again.

"You mean, you really are a vagrant? I don't believe it. Not a sweet thing like you."

"Only temporarily." Sherry shrugged.

"Her father kicked her out of her house," Mike said. Ignoring Sherry's protests, he explained her situation in a few succinct sentences.

"Oh, you poor thing." Clara squeezed Sherry's hand tight. "Well, that settles it."

"What settles what?" Mike appeared in the doorway. "Anybody want breakfast?"

Sherry glanced at Clara, then back at Mike. He cooked, too? "I could eat," she said.

She helped Clara stand and Mike came over to provide support on the long journey from living room to kitchen.

"Sherry has to stay here with us," Clara said.

"I can't do that," Sherry protested. "One night was more than enough."

"I don't mean here at Micah's. Unless you really want to." Clara winked at her again. "Stay with me next door. Until you can find a place of your own."

"Oh, no. I couldn't impose. Tell her, Micah. Mike."

Mike gave her a long, measuring look, long enough that she started to fidget. "I think it's a good idea," he said finally.

Three

Sherry stared at him, surprised. She had been given the distinct impression that this was a one-night-only deal. What had changed his mind?

He eased Clara down into a kitchen chair, ignoring her hands trying to slap him away.

"Stop fussing," Clara complained. "I'm not an invalid."

"Yes, you are." Mike propped his hands on his hips and looked at Sherry. "It would be a big help if I had someone to keep an eye on her while I'm at work. Someone to make sure she doesn't do things she's not supposed to do. Like sneak over to my kitchen and cook pot roast."

"Well, what am I supposed to do with myself?" Clara demanded. "Sit around and rot?"

"I need to find a job." Sherry didn't want to get into the middle of this family quarrel. "Find a place to live, that sort of thing."

"I'm shorthanded just now at the club. I can give you a job there, if you're interested. Daylight hours so you can mom-sit while I'm working. She just needs company."

"Stop talking about me like I'm not here." Clara punched him on the arm, then looked at Sherry. "Stay with me. If you rent an apartment, you have to give them an application fee and a deposit and the first month's rent and your firstborn child and—"

"Hey, I'm not that bad," Mike protested. "I don't want the kid. Just first and last month's rent. And an arm *or* a leg. Not both."

"You manage this place, too?" Sherry looked around, impressed. Mike Scott was an enterprising man.

He gave her an assessing look. "Yeah. That way the owner gives me a break on the rent, so I can afford two apartments. Mom refuses to live with me."

"A man needs his space," Clara said, sounding as if she'd said it many times before. "And Sherry needs a place to live."

"Okay, okay." Sherry held up her hands, laughing. "Now I see where your son got all his stubborn."

"I need it, handling her," Mike said.

"Who's the mother here, and who is the son?" Clara retorted.

Mike set a bowl of hot cereal in front of her. "Eat your breakfast."

"I already ate." But she picked up the spoon and stirred.

Mike set two plates of scrambled eggs and toast on the table for himself and Sherry, then poured coffee.

"You see how he treats me?" Clara pointed her spoon at the eggs. "Starving me to death. Won't even let me have one measly little egg—"

"They're bad for you, and you know it." Mike gestured for Sherry to sit down. "Quit complaining."

"What? And deprive myself of the last bit of entertainment left in my life?"

Sherry ate the food Mike had prepared, wallowing in the atmosphere as she listened to the affectionate bickering between Mike and his mother. Meals in the Nyland household had usually occurred either in grand isolation, everyone eating at different times, or in the middle of a screaming fight between Tug and Bebe that usually ended in someone throwing breakables. Their primary entertainment seemed to be quarreling. Sometimes Sherry and Juliana managed to eat together without the parents, but not often, given Juliana's busy social schedule.

"So," Sherry said as she helped clear away the dishes after Clara had been helped back into the living room. "When do I start work?"

Mike glanced at her before opening the dishwasher. "I usually go in about six, so—"

"No, I mean work work." Keeping company with Clara would be fun; but Sherry didn't think it would contribute much toward attaining her independence. "You did mean it when you offered me a job at La Jolie, didn't you?"

"I don't say things I don't mean." Mike stopped work and turned to stare at her, face calm, but the storm-cloud gray of his eyes hinted at his reaction to her unintended insult. "You sure you want to go in today? You had a pretty late night."

"I'm awake now. I'm perfectly capable of working. Why not start today? Unless—is there some kind of uniform I need to go get first?" If so, she hoped her cash would cover it.

"Hosts wear street clothes. Business clothes." He turned his attention back to the dishes. "I start everybody there, regardless of experience. Gives people a chance to learn the layout, the menu and how I like things to operate."

"Great. When do I start?"

He looked at his watch. "As soon as you change into something more businesslike than Tweety bird. Doors open at eleven. That should give you just enough time to take care of paperwork and learn where everything is."

Sherry turned her best smile on her new boss. This was going to work. Even the biggest gazillionaires had to start somewhere, right?

Mike grinned back. "Smile like that at the customers, and you'll make out just fine."

Leora had added a knit navy jacket with matching pink dress to the bag she'd packed for Sherry, which would have to do for "businesslike." It was all she had. Mike drove her the mile or so up the island to the club and introduced her to the day manager.

Sherry watched, but didn't see any of those sidelong, smirky looks that often showed up when people thought there was—as Clara put it—fun and frolic going on. Especially between boss and employee. Not that Sherry knew anything about boss-employee relations of any kind, not from personal experience, anyway. Mike had just given her her first job ever.

After quietly arranging to pick her up out front at the end of the day, Mike left Sherry to sink or swim on her own. She filled out half a dozen forms, met all the other employees whose names she promptly forgot, learned the table assigning system, and took position by the door to wait for the first customers of the day. She sincerely hoped that Alice, the day manager, meant it when she said she'd help as much as she could. With any luck, Sherry wouldn't cause any major disasters, like burning down the restaurant. Surely anything less would be forgivable. The front door opened and a cluster of lunching ladies clattered in.

Smile, Sherry reminded herself as she picked up her pencil. Mike's advice couldn't steer her wrong. "Four for lunch?"

* * *

The minute Mike turned on to the block at the end of the day, he saw Sherry waiting. She looked hot and tired, her skin shiny with sweat, her posture screaming weariness. He was impressed. Most people raised in her environment didn't have what it took to stick with a job that kept them on their feet all day. Sherry had stuck.

She got in the car, kicked her shoes off with a groan and slumped down in the seat, the way she had last night when she'd fallen asleep on the way home. What was it about bare feet? Her feet had been bare last night, and he'd seen them again this morning…when she came out of her bedroom wearing nothing but a T-shirt.

Mike rubbed his eyes, hoping to rub away the memory of the vision. Didn't work. Especially when she sat right next to him in a sleeveless pink dress that hugged every curve, easily seen now that the concealing navy jacket was rolled up in her lap. He pulled into traffic.

"How'd it go?" he said, partly to distract himself and partly because he wanted to know.

"I swear, if one more person pats me on the hand and tells me this job is 'beneath me' and that I should quit and run home to Daddy and my trust fund, I am going to scream." She blew a strand of hair out of her face, then pulled all her hair severely back from her face. "Maybe I should have put my hair up. What do you think? More businesslike? It's bound to be cooler."

Mike glanced at her and shrugged. "I'm not exactly an expert on hairstyles." Scraping her hair back that way made her look younger, more vulnerable.

"Maybe I'll just cut it all off."

"Suit yourself." He could feel her look at him, but resisted looking back. He had to keep his eyes on the road. And off Miss Nyland.

"That's an enlightened attitude," she said. "Most of the

men I know would put their foot down and absolutely forbid the idea.'' She made her voice go gruff and pompous on the last few words.

"It's *your* hair.''

"That's right. It is.'' She sighed and leaned her head back against the headrest. "I never knew hostessing was such hard work. I guess I would have if I'd thought about it, but I never did.''

Mike dared to look at her again. She looked exhausted and disheartened. Deliberately he reached over and patted her hand. "Don't worry,'' he said. "If you don't like the job, you always have your trust fund to fall back on.''

Sherry stared at him, eyes wide, mouth open in astonishment. Mike had to bite his lip to keep from laughing at her. Then devilment appeared in her eyes. She sat up straight, threw her head back and screamed.

The scream lasted a good fifteen, twenty seconds, loud and long. When she finished, Mike stuck a finger in his ear to see if he could bring his hearing back, and shook his head to clear it. "Feel better?''

She blinked and tipped her head, as if she was thinking about it. "Actually, yes. I do.''

He grinned at the surprise in her voice, and after a minute she grinned back. "Never cut loose like that before, huh?'' he said.

"Not like that. I guess the 'code' was ingrained too deep. You can drink yourself senseless, snort yourself silly and screw the help, but don't make a scene.'' Sherry put her feet up on the dashboard and curled her toes.

Mike glued his eyes to the road, but not before he got a good look at her forever legs with the pink dress sliding up them.

He'd seen those legs before, of course. She'd worn shorts last night and this morning. He'd thought at first that the Tweety T-shirt was her only covering, till it hiked up on one side to show the white shorts. She might as well not have worn them. They were *very* short shorts above *very* long legs. He was developing something of an obsession about those legs.

"So, did you?" he asked.

She opened her eyes and looked at him. "Did I what?" Her feet were on the floorboard again. Mike didn't know whether he was grateful or disappointed. Both, he decided.

"Screw the help."

"No, I did not!"

He had to laugh at her indignation, and she hit him. Thumped him on the arm the way his mom did.

"Oh!" Her hands flew to her mouth in horror. "I'm sorry. I shouldn't have—I never— Oh, I am so sorry."

Mike's chuckle trailed off. She was truly horrified that she had hit him. "Hey, it's okay. Don't worry about it. You were provoked."

"That's no excuse."

"You didn't hurt me. You couldn't, no matter how hard you hit."

She slanted a dirty look at him. Somehow that seemed dirtier than the straight-on dirty looks.

"Okay, maybe you could. A little," he conceded. "But it's nothing to get all bent out of shape about. Mom hits me like that all the time. You saw her."

"She's a frail old lady."

"She's a mean old broad." Mike grinned. "She's a bad example. Maybe you shouldn't stay with her. You're bound to pick up all kinds of bad habits. Beating people up. Breaking and entering. Surreptitious pot-roast cooking."

"Oh, shut up." Sherry still had her arms crossed, but Mike could see the smile flickering as he pulled into the garage.

"I moved your stuff over to Mom's place already," he

said on the elevator. He led the way down the hall and opened the door. "Honey, we're home!"

He sniffed. Good. No cooking smells. Maybe she would behave herself tonight. Clara sat tipped back in her recliner, her eyes still closed.

"Mom?"

She didn't move. Mike didn't know whether to swear or worry. If she was playing possum again... He hurried over to her and knelt by her chair. "Mom?" He picked her hand up and patted it.

"Is she all right?" Sherry's voice shook, her concern genuine.

Mike lowered his voice for his mom's ears only. "If you're playing games here, you'd better stop right now, or I swear you'll be eating tofu all week." Nothing. She didn't even seem to be breathing. "You're going to scare her off, Mom. Sherry thinks you're really sick."

At that, her eyelids fluttered, and Mike's heart started beating again. Every time she pulled her little game, he thought this time it might be real. He'd throttle her, if he didn't object to giving her the satisfaction of knowing she got to him. That was why he didn't swear the way he wanted to just now.

His mom's eyes opened and she gave a little fake yawn. "Oh, me, I must have fallen asleep. You're back already? Sherry, dear, how was the job?"

"Just fine, Mrs. Scott."

"Now what did I tell you to call me?"

Sherry beamed that glowing smile Mike wished she'd turn his way. No, he didn't. He didn't want anything from her but a little mom-sitting. She could save the smile for the customers, and Mom.

"Clara."

"That's better." She patted Sherry's hand. "Don't you worry about a thing. It'll all work out."

Sherry's smile got even bigger. "Thanks, Clara. I'm sure it will."

Mike rolled his eyes. "Well, since you two have your little mutual admiration society going here, I guess I'll go get ready for work."

They didn't so much as blink when he left.

Sherry had more fun keeping Mike's mother company than she'd had in a long time. Maybe ever. At least since her own mother died. She did remember a few good times from back then. But her time with Clara was definitely the best since. They looked at old photo albums, while Clara told stories about the mischief Mike had gotten into as a child.

Finally they put the albums on the shelf beneath the coffee table. "That was fun," Clara said. "But it's time to get serious. It's time to eat."

"What would you like?" Sherry reached for the phone book. When she'd informed Mike earlier that she didn't cook, he had told her to call La Jolie and have something healthy delivered. Besides the regular menu selections, his chefs always had healthy specials. It was one of the things that made La Jolie popular among the older, richer Palm Beach set.

"None of that rabbit food." Clara worked her way out of the chair to her feet. "Let's see what there is to cook."

"Clara, you heard what Mike said. You don't need to be on your feet for so long." Sherry took the frail woman's arm and walked with her into the kitchen, unable to stop her determined progress.

"Oh, I'm not cooking. You are."

"I can't cook!" Panic began to simmer inside Sherry. "I don't know how. I never had to."

"Well, don't you think it's time you learned?" Clara sat in a wooden chair in a room the mirror image of Mike's kitchen, right down to the black-and-white-checked floor tile and granite-topped cabinets. "I'll just sit here and tell you what to do."

Clara seemed so out of breath, Sherry ran back into the living room and got her oxygen. Clara took a few breaths from the mask, then smiled. "Thank you, dear. I tend to be a little more tired in the evenings."

"Are you sure you're okay?" Sherry hovered, her panic rising. She didn't want to kill Mike's mother the first night she stayed with her. She didn't want to lose this bright friendship before it had even begun.

"I'm fine. Go see what I have in the freezer." Clara pointed and Sherry went.

As she followed Clara's instructions, thawing a piece of snapper in the microwave, putting water on to boil for rice, Sherry began to believe she might actually be able to cook without making a total muddle of things.

"I'm not really trying to torture Micah, you know," Clara said, "when I pretend to be dead."

The abrupt change in the conversation startled Sherry. "You weren't asleep?"

"Your water's boiling. Pour the rice in and put the lid on, then turn the fire down low. Yes, that's right." Clara nodded as Sherry did as she was told. Then she sighed. "Not pretending exactly. More like—practicing. Or maybe hoping."

The tears in Clara's eyes worried Sherry, and she came to sit beside the older woman.

"I'm just so tired," Clara said. "And I miss Roger so terribly. I'm ready to be with him again. But I can't leave Micah, yet. He's not ready. He's so alone."

"He loves you."

"I know." Clara patted Sherry's hand, comforting her, instead of the other way round. "But I'm his mother. He needs someone of his own to love."

Sherry read the hope in Clara's eyes and shook her head. "I'm not that person. He can barely tolerate me."

"He likes you. I can tell." Clara pulled back her hand, then lifted both in a warding-off gesture. "Oh, I know. I'm being a meddling old fool. I'll stop. But I'd like to wring that spoiled brat's neck." Her eyes narrowed, and her hands made twisting motions in the air.

Sherry watched, fascinated. She'd never seen anyone speak so eloquently with hand motions.

"I just want to pop her little head right off," Clara said. "She ruined him, you know. Broke his heart. And now he won't even try."

"Who? Mike?"

"Well, who else have we been talking about?"

"What happened?" Sherry asked, curiosity aroused in spite of her best intentions.

"That's not my story to tell." Clara waved her away. "Go check on the fish. It broils fast."

Sherry felt like growling herself. But she didn't. It was none of her business whether Mike's heart was broken. Nor was his supposed loneliness any of her business. Just because so much of her own life had been spent drowning in loneliness didn't mean they had anything in common. It didn't mean they were the answer to each other's problem. It didn't mean anything, at all....

Dinner proved astonishingly delicious. Afterward, Sherry settled Clara in her recliner with the TV remote and cleaned up the kitchen. She had a little trouble figuring out how to load the dishwasher. It looked a little strange when she was done, but with any luck, the dishes would still get clean. When she returned to the living room, Clara had drifted to sleep to the sound of some raucous comedy.

Sherry was thumbing through old copies of *Southern Living* and resisting the urge to look at the photos again when the phone rang. Probably Mike, checking to see how things were going.

"Scott residence. Who's calling please?" she said in her best Easton School for Girls voice.

"Sherry? Is that you?" Definitely not Mike.

"Juliana? How did you get this number?" Why would her sister be calling? Sherry took the phone into the kitchen to keep from disturbing Clara. "What do you want? Did Tug put you up to—"

"Tug doesn't know anything about this. I just wanted to be sure you were okay." Juliana sounded worried. Sherry didn't want to worry her more. Her sister was sweet and shy and couldn't do anything to help.

"I'm fine. How did you get this number?"

"From Tug. From his desk. He doesn't know I have it."

"But how did he get it?" Dread settled over Sherry's shoulders.

"I don't really know. Does it matter? What's going on, Sherry? Why did you leave?"

"I'm going to live in the real world, kid. It's time, don't you think?" She needed to change the subject. "What's going on with you?"

"I think I'm getting married."

"What? What do you mean, you *think* you're getting married?"

"It's not definite." Juliana paused, and when she went on, her voice had faded, as if she were embarrassed. "One of those arranged things."

Now Sherry was worried. Surely Tug wasn't pulling the same trick on Juliana? She was the favorite daughter, the pride and joy. Then again, maybe Tug thought he could count on Juliana not to refuse. "You're not going through with it, are you?"

"I think I am. If he wants to. It's Kurt Collier, Sherry. At the very least, I want the chance to be engaged to him for a little while, to have a gorgeous man like him paying attention to me. If he pays attention to me."

And there was the difference between the daughters. Juliana got a marriage arranged with handsome, debonair Kurt Collier. Sherry got a marriage arranged with fish-lipped, frightening Vernon the Geek.

"You be careful, Julie." She used the old pet name. "Don't get in over your head."

A breathy laugh came over the phone. "It may be too late for that. I mean, *me?* With a man like *that?* How can I not get in over my head? I'll just have to keep telling myself 'It's just business, it's not real,' and keep paddling as fast as I can. What else can I do?"

"Don't let Tug and Bebe push you into anything. You can come stay with me if you need to."

"Thanks, Sher, but I don't think it's necessary."

"Are the parents the same?"

"Tug was pretty mad when you ran away."

She didn't exactly run away, but Sherry didn't see any reason to burden Juliana with the truth. Not yet, anyway. Maybe later, if the situation changed. "Has he calmed down, yet?"

Juliana hesitated before speaking. "Not really. He's still mad. I heard him yelling at somebody on the phone about you earlier. He said he knew where you were. That's why I came in to look for your phone number. Are you sure you're okay? Where are you staying?"

"With a very nice elderly lady. I'm helping to take care of her. And I'm fine. Honestly."

"Stay that way. Call me and let me know how you are. You're the only sister I've got, you know."

"I know. You be careful, Juliana. Hear me?"

"You be careful, too. Tug sounded awful mad. Scary."

"I will. Promise." Sherry carried the phone back to the

living room and set it gently in the base, glancing to see if Clara was still asleep, hoping she was.

The news that her father knew where to find her unnerved Sherry. No, it flat-out frightened her. Tug must have gone off some deep end. Locking her out of the house was extreme behavior, but what Juliana had described seemed to go further.

What if Tug came up to Clara's looking for Sherry? When he was in a temper, he had a lot in common with a bull in a china shop. He'd knock Clara over without even thinking about it. Frail as she was, any fall could break a hip. Plus she had that bad heart. A severe fright could be fatal. Though Clara didn't seem to fear much of anything, from what Sherry could tell. She'd be more likely to become so angry she'd have a heart attack. Sherry didn't much like the idea either way.

She needed a way to convince Tug to leave her alone. She could move out, keep him from Clara that way, but without transportation or any way to pay for an apartment, she had nowhere to go and no way to get there. If only she could buy some time.

In a few more months—three months and sixteen days, to be exact—she would turn twenty-five and gain control of the trust fund her mother had left her. Then she would have plenty of money to do whatever she wanted. But with Tug on the rampage, she didn't know if she could wait it out.

She had never seen him so out of control. Then again, Tug had never seemed to be under this much stress before. The arguments between Tug and her stepmother, Bebe, had always been a constant, but the tone had become much more strident, more angry over the past few months. Sherry had figured out the reason when she'd started answering phone calls from creditors dunning for payment.

Somehow Tug and Bebe must have gone through all

their piles of money. They still owned the house and all its
fabulous holdings; but God forbid that they sell anything,
or stop buying new items. Appearances must be kept up,
after all. Sherry figured that was why Tug had come up
with his brilliant daughter-auction idea. He had to be getting desperate.

Still, she didn't believe he would go so far as physical
violence. If he did anything to Sherry, he couldn't marry
her off. When he locked her out of the house, he had obviously expected her to come running back begging to do
whatever he wanted. But she hadn't. What tactics might he
resort to next? Kidnapping?

Sherry couldn't see Tug giving up on his insane plan.
Unless she took herself off the market. He couldn't marry
her to Vernon…if she were already married to someone
else.

Four

Mike got home not long after midnight, leaving a little early so he could check on how things went with his mom and Miss Nyland—Miss Nyland who was now sitting cross-legged on the floor outside his apartment in her tiny white shorts and a tiny blue top. Didn't she own anything that covered more skin?

"Anything wrong?" he asked, striding down the hall in a hurry. "Is Mom okay? I left numbers for you to call—"

"She's fine. Sleeping like a baby. Better. She doesn't wake up and cry."

He slowed his pace. He wanted to keep hurrying till he reached her side, but he didn't want to want it, so he dawdled. "What brings you out here, then? You've got work again tomorrow. It's a little late, isn't it?"

"Earlier than we got in last night."

"True." Mike stopped in the hallway, looking down at her, resisting the urge to reach down and lift her to her feet.

She was farther away sitting on the floor. "Did you want something?"

Sherry took a deep breath. Mike didn't watch the way it made her breasts rise and fall beneath the snug-fitting top. Not much.

"I wanted to talk to you," she said. "I have a proposition to make."

"Sounds serious."

And she looked so cute. He wanted to smile, just looking at her, but she'd probably think he was laughing at her. Besides, why should he smile? She was a Palm Beach trust-fund baby with no idea of what life was like in the real world and no interest in finding out. This was just temporary, as she said. Just a phase brought on by desperation, because she didn't like the rich geek Daddy picked out. She'd find a guy with lots of money who suited her better, and Micah Scott wouldn't even be a fond memory.

But he could see something in her expression, or maybe in her eyes. Fear? "Come on." He held his hand out to her. "We can talk inside. I never discuss propositions in public."

Sherry took his hand and let him pull her to her feet. He unlocked the door and ushered her into his bachelor quarters for the second time.

"So," he said. "What's up?"

"Mike?" She twisted her hands together, like she wanted to tie them in knots.

"Yeah?" What could have her in such a dither?

"Will you please marry me?"

Mike stared at her. He closed his eyes, then opened them again, in case this was some weird hallucination, but she was still there. Still twisting her hands together, looking anxious.

"Come again?" he said. Surely he couldn't have heard her right. He tilted his head to hear better.

"Will you marry me?" Sherry started to pace along with the hand twisting. "I know it sounds crazy, but it's the only way."

"The only way to what? Get yourself locked up in the nuthouse?"

"Don't use that word."

"What word? Nuthouse? Honey, if the shoe fits..."

"Don't call me honey, either."

"Why not? You just asked me to marry you. Honey." Now he was pacing, at right angles to Sherry. Her pacing had rubbed off on him.

"Because you don't mean it." She stopped to watch him walk back and forth. "Besides, I didn't really ask you to marry me."

"You didn't? Gee, that's what it sounded like to me. What did you say? 'Mike, will you please marry me?' Yep. That sounds a hell of a lot like a proposal to me. Note I said proposal and not proposition."

"If you'll just calm down and let me explain, you'll see that it's not really such a big thing."

"It sounds like a big thing to me. A damn big thing."

"Mike, please."

The plea in her voice made him stop. He turned to face her, arms crossed. She couldn't possibly have any explanation that would make sense, that could make him agree to such a whacked-out idea. Even if the idea of snuggling up every night to Miss Sherry Nyland's sweet curves had him breaking out in "want-to" hives, he couldn't do it, precisely because the idea held so much appeal.

But he would listen. She was obviously worried about something. He could at least find out what it was. "All right, talk."

"I got a call this evening from Juliana. She called your mother's number. She got it off my father's desk. I don't know how he got it—probably somebody who was in the club today called and told my father I was working there, though how he got Clara's home number, I don't know. But I know Tug has the phone number. And the address.''

Mike swore. He didn't know Sherry's father, but he didn't like the idea of a guy who would kick his own daughter out on the street knowing where his mom lived, no matter how good the security was here. ''What does that have to do with you wanting to marry me? Is it money?''

She frowned. ''I'm not exactly sure. Probably. It has to be. Why else…?''

''How can you not know? Either you want the money or you don't.'' He advanced on her, angry. These trust-fund kids were all the same. Damn her for proving it. Damn him for wanting her anyway.

Sherry backed away, putting her hands over her ears. ''Stop distracting me. You keep talking and it gets me off-track. Just let me explain, okay?''

''Okay.'' Mike glared down at her, hands on his hips.

She ducked away from him, crossing the room to start her pacing again. ''Juliana told me she heard Tug shouting today. Yelling on the phone at somebody.''

''What does that have to do with you wanting to marry me?''

''I don't think either Tug or Vernon is going to back down till they get what they want. Which is me, married to Vernon. I don't know exactly why they're so determined, but it has to have something to do with money. I think— I'm not sure—but I *think* Vernon must be paying money to Tug so I'll marry him. I don't know why he'd want to do a crazy thing like that, but that's the only reason that occurs to me.''

Mike knew why, running his gaze over her sleek figure and classically beautiful face, but if she didn't know, he wasn't going to be the one to tell her.

''But if I'm married to someone else,'' she went on,

"then obviously I can't be married to Vernon. All I need is to be married till I turn twenty-five. Then we can get a divorce."

"What's so important about twenty-five?"

"That's when I get control of my trust fund."

"I knew it!" Mike bit out a curse. He'd hoped, just a little, that Sherry might somehow be different. He should have known better.

"I just need some time. I need to get Tug to back off till I can get my trust fund. There's twenty million there, more or less. I can make it worth your while to do this for me."

Mike went cold inside. He shouldn't. He already knew the truth. In her circles, money always came first. This time she was offering him money instead of expecting to get it from her, but it made him feel the same way. He stalked toward her, advancing as she backed away, until he had her backed into a corner. "Is that what you think?" He kept his voice soft. "That I can be bought with your money?"

"No." She came back at him. "I'm not that way, either. I won't be sold."

"Why not? That's what your kind does, isn't it?" Mike backed off a few paces, disturbed by the attraction he still felt. "Buy and sell each other, have mergers instead of marriages?"

"Maybe. Some of them. But not me."

"Sure. Tell me another one. Tell me the only reason you just asked me to marry you isn't to protect that precious trust fund. So you'll have money after you reach that magic birthday."

"The money isn't important, except that it will allow me to get them off my back. I'll be able to get a place to live with good security, get a car—or hire somebody to get my car back for me. My name is on the title."

"You don't need money to do that. Report it stolen."

"Really?" Sherry sounded surprised, but she shook it off, going back to her purpose. "My car isn't the point here."

"You're right. Money is."

She sighed. "Money is nothing more than a tool. The point is that my father wants me to marry Vernon Greeley, and I'm not sure how far he will go to get what he wants."

He frowned. "As far as violence?"

"I don't know. I don't think so, but—" Sherry wrapped her arms around herself, suddenly looking small and fragile. "I just don't know."

Mike started pacing again and ran a hand back over his hair. He didn't dare let himself believe her. He'd been down that road before. And yet her story sounded plausible, given what he already knew.

"I don't understand." He shook his head. "You would rather sleep on the beach than marry this Vernon guy in a business arrangement. But now you want to do the same thing with me."

"It's not the same thing."

"No? What's the difference?"

"You're not Vernon."

"You think I'd be easier to control? Is that it?" He slapped a hand against the wall, hard enough to rattle the family pictures hanging there, before turning to pace the other way, toward Sherry. "Do you think you can shut the bedroom door and I'll stay out? That works when you're a house guest, little girl, but not if you're my wife."

Mike caught her wrist and pulled her hard against him. He kept hold of her wrist as his arm went around her, pinning it behind her. His other hand stabbed into her hair, gripping her head as he took what he had wanted since he'd first seen her.

He started with a kiss, openmouthed and demanding.

Sherry stiffened and he bent her back over his arm, ready to batter down her defenses. Then she melted against him.

Her hand, the one he didn't hold captive, slid up his back, and her fingernails dug in. Her mouth softened, opened, welcomed him, gave what he demanded. When he rocked his hips against her, hers rocked back. The kiss he'd intended as punishment transformed into passion, and he lost himself in it. In her.

Mike slid his hand from her hair down to stroke the smooth graceful column of her neck and was moving lower when he caught himself. This wasn't what he wanted.

He'd wanted to scare her off, and instead he'd scared himself. He'd only known her twenty-four hours, but he knew already this was a woman he could fall hard for. He couldn't do it again. He wouldn't survive a second time, and he knew, as well as he knew his own name, that anything he could have with Miss Sherry Eloise Nyland wouldn't last. She believed he was just a working stiff, living from paycheck to paycheck. She was slumming. Trying out a new plaything. Her attitude might change if she knew he probably had more money than she did, but that would be even worse. He couldn't do what she asked, and he could never, ever kiss her again.

He set her a few steps away from him. "It wouldn't work."

"It…" Sherry swayed, her eyes glazed over. She licked her lips. Mike stifled his groan.

"I wouldn't mind," she said. "If you wanted—you know—sex. It would be all right."

She was making him crazy. Mike ran both hands back over his hair, one after the other. "Why me? Why me and not Vernon?" He needed to know.

"I trust you. You're a good man. Vernon…isn't."

Mike stopped in midpace and turned to look at her.

"What do you mean?" He didn't like the way she'd said that.

"I—" She was back to the hand twisting again. "I'm not sure, exactly. It's hard to explain. People talk about how brown eyes look so warm and kind, but Vernon's don't. They're cold. Hard. He looks at me like I'm a bug and not a person. Or maybe it's more like I'm like a toy he wants to play with. I'm just a thing to Vernon. And he pinches."

Sherry lifted her arm, turning it to show the tender upper inside surface. Half a dozen tiny yellow-green bruises marred her perfect skin.

Anger blasted through Mike. Who the hell did this joker think he was?

"He scares me, Mike." She folded her arms protectively across her chest.

"He won't touch you again." Mike cradled her against him, stroking her hair until she relaxed and let her head settle against his shoulder. He ignored the way she fit there, just like he ignored the urge to pull her hard against his arousal. He was above his urges, smarter than his hormones.

"Then you'll marry me?"

"No. But I'll protect you."

Her head came up and she looked at him, her eyes suspiciously shiny. "How? You have to work. So do I."

"I seriously doubt they're going to try to snatch you off the street or out of the club." Most Palm Beach types didn't have the guts for something like that.

"But what if they do? Juliana said Tug sounded furious. Mad enough to scare her."

"I can put you on nights, when I'm there. If he's desperate, he'll do something soon. I can play bodyguard a day or two."

"What about your mother? You need me here when

you're at work. And if they came looking for me here, I can just see her losing her temper right into a coronary. I know the building has pretty good security, but no security is perfect. I don't want her hurt.''

Neither did Mike. ''She can go stay with one of my sisters till things calm down.''

Sherry bit her lip. He wished she wouldn't do that. ''What if they don't calm down? I'm really afraid that if I'm not actually married…''

''It won't come to that. But if it does, you can decide what to do then.'' He gave her a quick squeeze and stepped away, reaching for distance. ''It'll be okay. Promise.''

He only hoped it was a promise he could keep.

The next day, after an all-morning ''discussion'' with Clara about the situation, Sherry helped Clara pack, while Mike made arrangements with his sister. Although she didn't know this sister, Sherry was pretty sure Mike had given her the harder job, because Clara was unpacking almost as fast as Sherry could pack. Things went faster when Mike came in to pack his mother's medication and Clara left to undo her son's work.

Sherry put in the last pair of support stockings, closed the suitcase and latched it. Good thing Clara's son had muscles, Sherry thought as she hefted it off the bed. The suitcase had to weigh a couple of tons. Her assigned task finished, all the second thoughts and misgivings rushed in on her again.

For somebody who claimed to want independence, asking a perfect stranger to marry her didn't exactly seem the best way to go about it. But then, independence wasn't exactly the right word for what she wanted. She knew better than to think she could stand by herself in absolute self-sufficiency. Nobody could do everything all alone without any assistance ever.

So she needed a little temporary help. So she asked Mike to marry her. So what? It didn't mean she was in love with him. That kiss didn't mean he was in love with her, either. He only kissed her to try to scare her off. She just had to forget the way it sizzled all the way through to every tiny capillary in her body.

They weren't in love, and it was better that way. Much better. Nobody would get hurt. She was never ever again going to love anybody who didn't love her back, and Mike didn't. He was still going to help her, even though he'd turned down her marriage idea. Only, now she felt guilty for putting him to all this trouble.

"Everything okay in here?" Mike's voice behind her made her jump.

Sherry pasted on her brightest smile. "All done. It was easy once you distracted Clara."

"I should've said, 'Are *you* okay?'" He came in the room, shrinking it by at least half. "I couldn't help but notice you looked worried." His hand rose, as if to touch her, but stalled out before it arrived. "You don't have to worry about your father. He won't bother you. And if he does, I'll be there."

Sherry bit her lip. "Are you sure? I can't help but think your life would be a lot simpler if you just showed me the door and waved goodbye."

His grin didn't help matters. "Now, why would I want to do that?"

"I can't believe you have to ask. I've disrupted your whole life. You're moving your mother out of her home. I won't be able to stay with her, which is why you asked me to stay in the first place—"

"No." Mike touched a finger to Sherry's mouth, stopping her tumble of words. "I asked you to stay because you didn't have anywhere else to go."

Even so brief a touch burned, but his kindness burned

deeper. Tears welled up in her eyes and she fought them back. "Why are you being so nice to me? You don't even know me."

"You're my employee—"

"Which I wouldn't be if you hadn't been so nice."

"You work for me." Mike spoke over her last words, his voice hard, emphatic. "I take care of my people because they work hard for me."

"I bet you don't invite them all home to stay with your mother."

Again his teasing grin came back. "That's because she scares them all off. Believe me, I've tried. She likes you. If I waved goodbye, she'd make my life a living hell. You think she's bad now, you should see her when she's really trying."

He touched her arm, urging her toward the door. "I said I'd help you and I will. I don't go back on my word."

"Even if it's the smart thing to do?"

"Even if." Mike picked up the suitcase. "Maybe it's not the smart thing, but it's the right thing to do. Come on. Let's get Mom moved."

"Why don't I just wait here? You don't need me sticking my nose in your family business. Not any more than it already is." She felt awkward with the situation.

"I don't want you staying here by yourself." He herded Sherry ahead of him. "Not until we know for sure what your father intends. Probably nothing, but I don't want to take the chance. Besides, I need you to carry Mom's medicine. I've got my hands full with Mom and the rest of her stuff. Maybe if we're lucky, any people who see our trek across the lobby will think you're moving on and tell your dad."

Not one to keep fighting when she'd so obviously lost, Sherry picked up the train case of medications from the dresser by the door and followed along behind, trying to hide her amusement at Clara's continuing ploys to get out of the move.

Mike saw his mother safely installed in his oldest sister's house in West Palm Beach after a litany of complaints and excuses all the way there and after arriving. Nothing new there. On the way back to the island, his cell phone rang.

"Micah Scott." He identified himself. Had to be business. Nobody else ever called.

"This is Alice."

He sat up straight. Alice never called unless something important came up, and she was a good judge of the important. "What's up?"

"You said to call if somebody came around asking about the new girl. Sherry, right?"

Chills danced little goose feet down his spine. "That's right." He pulled to a halt at a red light, resisting the urge to look at the young woman sitting in the seat beside him. He didn't want to alarm her if it wasn't necessary.

"And?" he prompted when Alice didn't continue.

"Somebody came. Big guy, middle-aged, blond hair, red face. He asked for Sherry. I told him she wasn't here. He asked if she worked here. I asked if he wanted a table for lunch. He left."

Now Mike looked at Sherry. "Is your father a big blond red-faced guy?"

"That's him." She frowned. "Why?"

"He came to the club looking for you. He left again, peacefully."

"More or less," Alice added, catching Mike's comment over the phone. "He yelled a little, but he didn't break anything."

"Do you think he'll be back?" Mike said, not sure which woman he asked.

"Couldn't say," Alice said.

"Probably." Sherry crossed her legs. Mike didn't look. Much. "Tug's hardheaded. If he gets an idea, he doesn't give it up easily. He may not be back today or even tomorrow. But I'm sure he'll be back."

"Thanks, Alice. Let me know if anything else happens."

"Sure thing, boss man."

Mike punched off the phone and slid it back into his shirt pocket. He still didn't think this guy, Sherry's father, had the nerve to do anything serious; but he was liking the picture he had of the guy less and less. "Maybe you should just stay home tonight."

"No." Sherry was already shaking her head. "I might have run, but I'm not hiding. Even though I can't stay with your mom for you, with all this going on, I am not going to leave you short-handed at your club, and I'm certainly not going to wimp out on the job after just one day."

He had to smile, in spite of knowing how dangerous it was. Everything she said made it harder for him to remember that she'd been born to millions, that she was just waiting to collect the millions tucked away for her birthday, and that those millions were the center around which her life revolved.

Maybe he should tell her about his own millions. Her behavior would instantly change, and he wouldn't be so tempted to like her. But as long as she didn't know, she wouldn't like him back, and as long as she didn't like him back, he ought to be okay.

"Since you'll be working nightshift with me," he said, "and it doesn't start for another four hours, is there anything you need to do before then, while we're out?"

She looked down at her shorts. Mike looked, too. Just a little bit.

"Shopping?" Sherry scrunched up her nose. There ought to be a law against pretty girls doing any nose scrunching.

"I've only got one dress. I should probably have at least one other outfit so I can wear one and wash the other."

That made him mad, the idea of Sherry locked out without any of her belongings. "We should go collect your things."

"Later, maybe." She gave a one-shouldered shrug. "I'm a big coward, okay? I'm afraid if I go back in that house—even with you along—I'll never get out again. And there would be yelling."

Mike nodded. He didn't much like it, but it was her choice. "Shopping, it is."

He drove to the nearest mall, sighing internally, where she wouldn't see it. Shopping was not exactly his favorite leisure-time activity, even for himself. Shopping with women rated right beside shaving with tweezers. Given the spontaneous nature of this expedition, the odds of Sherry running into trouble were minimal, but Mike still didn't like the idea of leaving her by herself. So he sighed in silence and resigned himself to an afternoon of…discomfort.

He followed her from store to store, avoiding, to his surprise, the pricier boutiques. Sherry seemed to concentrate on the sale racks, flipping quickly through the merchandise, pausing only occasionally to look at something more closely. As they departed the seventeenth store for the eighteenth, Mike couldn't hold back any longer. "Wasn't there anything worth buying?"

"Maybe." Sherry didn't seem to be aware she was talking to an actual other person. Her words sounded as if she were thinking aloud. "Those black silk-blend pants had possibilities. But they weren't marked down much. I ought to be able to find something better. Maybe."

Mike came to a stunned standstill. "Are you trying to tell me that you intend to visit every store in this mall before you buy anything?"

She blinked at him, as if only now realizing he was there.

"Well...yes. How else am I going to know who has the best stuff at the best price?" She tipped her head, obviously considering his frazzled state. "I did tell you to pick a spot and wait for me, remember?"

"And I told you why I couldn't do that. My reasons still hold." He shifted his weight from one abused foot to the other. "Why can't you just pick something out and buy it?"

"Because I've only got fifty-three dollars cash to go as far as I can make it stretch."

"What's wrong with plastic?"

She blinked at him. "Nothing. Except Tug canceled all my credit cards."

He should have expected her jerk-of-a-father to do something like that. Obviously, the shopping was interfering with his brain cells. It had to be, because otherwise he never would have said anything remotely resembling what came out of his mouth next. "Let me pay for it."

"No," she said. "Not just no, but hell, no."

He should have expected that, too. Sherry had argued with every suggestion he'd made so far today. In fact, she'd argued with him pretty much since they'd first met.

"Why not?" he said. "Look, it's worth it to me just to get out of here."

"Absolutely not." Sherry spun around and started marching down the mall again. "No. No way, no how, no— Just no. You're not going to do that. Period."

"Why not?" Now his knees were protesting along with his feet as he followed after her. It was purely psychological, he knew. He could shop for restaurant fixtures for hours on end. But trailing through five zillion dress departments was not fun. "Think of it as an advance on your salary if you want."

"Can you hear me? No." She turned to face him, exaggerating her lip action as she spoke. "Read my lips. No."

He'd rather kiss them. Especially now that he'd kissed her last night and knew just how spectacularly those lips kissed. Well enough to tie him into more knots than a Boy Scout practice rope. Which was why he couldn't kiss them again, and probably shouldn't even read them, given what reading them made him think.

He should just listen to the words coming out of them. She'd been talking all during his mental trip into the forbidden territory of Kissing Land. He figured he was a sentence behind, at the very least.

"...have done too much already," she was saying. Sounded like stuff he'd heard before. "I refuse to let you do more. I've messed up your life, kicked your mother out of—"

"She'll enjoy having a chance to torture Nina and her family," Mike interrupted. "She likes having fresh victims every now and then. Probably why she likes you."

Sherry kept going, as if he'd never spoken. "I'm even eating your mother's food, for heaven's sake. You've given me a place to stay. You've given me a job. You're not giving me anything else. Do you understand me?" Now she paused.

"Yes." Mike jumped in quickly, in case she was just stopping for a breath. "But would you give me something? Like, a break? Out of all the stuff you've seen in the fifty gazillion stores we've already been to, isn't there a great bargain in there somewhere? Can't you give me just a little, tiny break?"

She stared at him a second, then burst out laughing. "I shouldn't. I offered you an out earlier, remember, and you wouldn't take it. So I know that you know all your suffering is your own fault. Mostly." She sighed then. "Actually, it's mostly Tug's fault."

Mike wanted to banish the haunted look from her eyes,

but even if he knew how, he couldn't do it. He didn't dare get any more involved with her.

Sherry sighed again. "Too bad we can't torture Tug." She thought another moment, then a smile appeared, quickly growing into a grin. "Okay. You've given me the excuse. I still have to try on the pants, but if they fit, I'll buy them. And the blouse I saw in the first store we went to."

"Thank you." Mike led the way back into the store, though he knew for security reasons he ought to follow. But following meant watching her walk, and that led to fantasizing, which led to remembered kisses, which led to more fantasizing, which led into deep, deep trouble.

He didn't want to go there. Nor did he want to think about the disappointment he felt when Sherry refused his offer to spend money on her. He ought to be glad she refused. And he was. He liked knowing she wasn't interested solely in what he could give her. And yet, it stung a little—Sherry refusing his gift.

Still, she was right. He'd done enough. He couldn't afford to do any more. Oh, his wallet could afford almost anything. But she was definitely way too pricey for his peace of mind.

Five

Sherry's feet were killing her. The evening was winding down. The few stragglers still coming in for a very late dinner were far outnumbered by laughing groups looking for drinks and dessert, and well-dressed couples wanting a romantic corner and expensive wine. She had just seated a gaggle of tourists in the bar and was hurrying back to her post to help the quartet of blue-haired ladies in bright silk cocktail dresses when she was yanked off her feet.

She landed in the lap of a very drunk, very young man who still gripped her wrist, the one he'd grabbed to pull her down. She turned her head to escape his toxic breath and escaped the kiss he intended, as well. It landed mostly on her hair somewhere in the vicinity of her ear, and it made her flesh crawl.

"Join the party, babe!" The young man bellowing the words, the one who'd grabbed her, had no neck. Given that, his age and the jacket he wore proclaiming the name of a nearby university, Sherry surmised that he and his equally drunk companions were students at that university.

"No, thank you." She put all the icy reserve she could manage into her voice as she struggled to her feet. She'd learned through experience that coldness usually worked better than hot anger with drunks.

No-neck grinned, spreading his arms in a mockery of innocent fun. "Just trying to be sociable."

"Don't." Sherry stalked back to the door, hoping none of the other customers had paid any attention. At least he'd been cooperative. She hid the shaking of her hands by gripping the menus extrahard.

She tried to talk the blue-haired ladies into a table in the dining room, but they insisted on the bar, so she led them in a wide circle around the rowdy bunch. However, one lady in hot pink strayed too close. She jumped and squealed when one of the boys goosed her, but she didn't seem too offended. Sherry wondered if she might have strayed deliberately. Still, someone else would probably take serious offense.

On her return to the front, Sherry saw Bruno the bartender waving her over and went to see what he wanted. Mike had mentioned that Bruno would be helping to keep an eye out for trouble. Of course, they'd expected trouble from Tug, not a bunch of party-minded college students.

"You okay?" Bruno asked. "I saw what those jerks did."

"I'm fine." She glared at their table as they burst into raucous laughter. One of them saw her looking and pursed his lips into smacking air kisses. She shuddered, turning back to Bruno. "*They* may not be, if they try it again."

"I'm gonna get Mike down here." He picked up the in-house phone. "He doesn't like customers getting out of hand. This is supposed to be a place with class."

Sherry frowned. "What can he do?"

"Kick 'em out." Bruno smoothed away his frown and put on a BBC accent. "Excuse me. I mean, escort them from the premises."

That worried her a little. Mike was strong. She knew that. She'd seen his muscles, up close and personal. And wet, not to mention mostly naked. But never mind the muscles. There was only one of Mike and five of these guys. And they were big. And probably athletes. But maybe there wouldn't be a problem. Maybe they would go peacefully. And maybe it would snow tomorrow. In Palm Beach. In May.

"Don't worry," Bruno said as he hung up the phone. "Mike can handle it. He can handle pretty much anything. They won't bother you anymore."

"Is this a little hero worship I hear?" Sherry had to smile. Bruno and subtle weren't very well acquainted.

"He gave me a job in this classy place. He made sure I got one of the scholarships the company gives out. He lets me work my job schedule around my class schedule. And he's a babe magnet. What's not to worship?" Bruno grinned at her. "Especially since none of the babes stick. I can catch what he shakes off."

"Gee. Too bad I'm demagnetized. No sticking, no shaking, no catching." Sherry liked Mike. She admired him. She was grateful for his help. But none of it extended as far as magnetic attraction.

"In your case, *you're* the magnet." He tipped his head toward the young drunks. "Couldn't you tell?"

"What's the problem?" Mike materialized out of nowhere, lightly touching Sherry's elbow. "Are you all right?"

She eased away, unnerved by the little thrill that went through her at his touch. Gratitude, respect, liking. That was *all* she felt. Except for the urge to touch him all over, from the dimple in his cheek to the— Okay, it was all she *wanted* to feel. She smiled, hoping it would hide the unease. "Just fine. I've been handling drunks for years."

"While you're working here, I'd rather you left them to me." His smile flashed and vanished, reassuring her. Darn it. She didn't want to feel safer when he was around. She could not start thinking she needed him.

He squeezed her hand—more reassurance, darn it again—before starting across the room to the table in question.

"See?" Bruno's voice startled her. She'd forgotten he was there. "*You're* the magnet."

Sherry made a rude noise. Physical urges didn't mean anything. There was no magnetism going either direction. She wouldn't allow it. She straightened upright from a faint lean in Mike's direction the instant she realized she was doing it. "I have to get back to work."

"Right." Bruno winked at her.

She stuck her tongue out at him and marched back to the door, where fortunately no one was waiting. Okay, so Micah Scott was devilishly handsome as well as incredibly nice. That only meant he was fun to look at. No rules against looking, not even in the brand-new book of Sherry's *Rules for a New Life*. She could look. She just couldn't want.

Mike said something that didn't seem to go over well with the noisy group. One of them stood, glaring down at Mike's considerable height from a height even greater. Sherry watched, heart pounding. They were all so big. At least, so far, only one was physically challenging Mike's authority. So far.

Then with an almost invisible flicker of motion, things changed. The one boy's expression morphed from anger to pain as Mike held him in some hidden, obviously uncomfortable grip. The others transformed from belligerent defiance into uncertainty. Mike spoke again, tipping his head toward the door, and the four drunken men all stood in unison and trooped meekly in that direction.

"Sorry," no-neck mumbled as he passed Sherry.

She could only nod in acknowledgment, so firmly did shock hold her in its grip.

Mike escorted the boy he still held captive at the end of the line. "I'm sure you'll find the Cabana more to your liking. Just a few more blocks down the beach," Mike said, releasing his prisoner with a not-too-gentle push out the door.

"My, my. I am impressed." Sherry winced as she heard herself. That sounded snarky and sarcastic. Not how she felt. "I mean it." She tried to fix it. "I am really, very impressed. I was worried, just a little. I mean, five big jocks against just you?"

"You were worried? About me?" Mike settled his suit jacket back into place on his shoulders, then adjusted the sleeves, never taking his eyes off her.

Her correction sounded as if she cared, which she did, but not like *that*. She had to keep things light. Casual. Fluffy. Sherry shrugged. "Well, sure I did. If those guys had broken your neck, who would protect me from the big bad Tug?" She fluttered her eyelashes madly to show she was teasing.

Fortunately, he laughed. "I can handle myself."

"Even better, you could handle those guys. How did you learn how to do that?"

"I joined the marines out of high school—wasn't ready for any more school right then." His smile just touched his eyes. "I learned a lot of interesting things."

"You? A Marine?" Sherry surveyed his perfectly tailored charcoal-gray suit. Not designer or tailor-made, but still very nice. "I find that hard to believe."

"Hoo-rah," he said. "Got the tattoo and everything."

Her eyes narrowed. "So why didn't I see any tattoo

when, um, when…'' She couldn't actually mention the bathroom towel incident out loud with him looking at her.

He grinned big enough to blind her. ''Hmm. I don't know. Why didn't you? Could it be because you weren't looking at my arms?''

Sherry's face burned like fire. She wanted to stick her tongue out at him the way she had at Bruno, but Mike was the boss, not the bartender. Besides, she was pretty sure her tongue wasn't safe with Mike anywhere around. She hadn't forgotten that kiss, even if he apparently had.

He pointed to his left arm, just below the upper bulge of muscle. ''It's right there. 'Semper fi.' Want to see?''

The fire under her skin burned hotter. She knew her face had to match the lobsters served up in the dining room. ''No, thank you,'' she said primly. ''Not just now.''

His wicked grin didn't fade. ''I'll take that rain check.''

At long last the front door opened and a designer-dressed couple entered. Sherry turned to them with relief. She hadn't given Mike a rain check, had she? Yes, she had. Did that mean deep down she wanted to see his tattoo? Heaven help her, it probably did.

She smiled her brightest. ''Two? Smoking or non?''

Two days passed without any more trouble, and Mike started to relax. As much as it was possible to relax with a gorgeous, leggy blonde staying next door at his mother's place when his mother wasn't there to keep him honest. Right now he was less concerned for her safety than for his own. The way he'd manhandled the drunks who'd manhandled Sherry was a case in point.

She'd been fine, had dealt with the situation perfectly. But when Bruno told him what had happened, Mike's temper—the blinding rage he thought he'd learned to control years ago—hit flash point in about a millionth of a second. He'd wanted to hurt somebody, and he had. Not as much as he'd wanted to. Not as much as he could have. The kid would have shaken it off before he reached the dance club Mike had pointed them to. He'd maintained at least that much control.

But he'd still hurt the kid, and that bothered him. A lot. Because it meant that Sherry was getting to him. She was beginning to matter more than an employee ought to matter. She should be nothing more than your basic charity case, and she wasn't.

Mike was relieved her father hadn't turned up. After this long, he probably wouldn't. Mike would give it a few more days just to be sure. If nothing happened in that time frame, as he fully expected, then he'd bring his mom home and let Sherry go back on days so she could keep an eye on Clara, and Mike could start avoiding the woman. Maybe he could see about getting her car back for her, too, so he wouldn't have to keep playing chauffeur.

He was working on the business plan for the new restaurant he'd just bought into over in West Palm Beach. The Trangs were smart and worked hard, but they had needed a little more capital backing them up, and some help on the business side to make a real go of it. He figured they'd be ready to buy him out and take over alone in a couple of years. He'd make a tidy profit on the deal and have a little fun in the meantime.

He liked the challenge of getting a new place off the ground. By investing rather than buying it outright, he could do the part he liked and let his partners do the hard work. He'd done his share of it in the past, when he was just starting out. He'd made his money by buying businesses or buying into them, making them profitable, then selling them at a bigger profit. A small-scale version of the big corporation's mergers, only his seemed to work out better. Plenty of money could be made at his level. His bank accounts were proof. Just now he had pieces of more than a dozen businesses all over Florida, and somebody from Savannah had contacted him yesterday about a place there.

He was about to move on to the information he'd been sent about Chez Bubba, the Savannah restaurant, when the phone beeped. "Yeah?" he said, most of his attention on his papers.

"Better get down here fast, boss," Bruno said. "Looks like big trouble. Sherry—"

"I'm on my way." Mike tossed the phone in the direction of its cradle and blew out the door, cursing himself for worrying about his own problems instead of the vulnerable woman he'd promised to protect. He shouldn't have relaxed.

He skidded down the stairs, touching maybe three of them, and paused just inside the kitchen door to pull himself together fast. He straightened his tie and smoothed back his hair in a physical echo of the control he tried to assert over his temper. It wouldn't do to alarm the customers. And though he didn't yet know the exact nature of the trouble out front, he had a pretty good idea. If it was Sherry's father, Mike didn't want his own temper setting the guy off.

Sherry was nowhere in sight when Mike emerged from the kitchen. He fought down the alarm screaming in his brain and strode quickly to the bar.

Bruno met him halfway. "I was just about to go after her. The guy took Sherry outside. Big guy, older, blonde. She didn't want to go, but she didn't want to make a big scene."

Mike swore. "She should have. Okay, thanks, Bruno. I'll take it from here. You go back to work."

"Sure thing, Big Mike."

Out on the sidewalk, brightly lit by pinkish streetlights and the mellow glow of the club's lighting, Mike saw them.

Sherry had her heels dug in, pulling back against the man's grip on her arm as he tried to lead her to a big black luxury car parked at the curb.

"Sherry, is this man bothering you?" Mike stepped into their path.

"Yes. Yes, he is."

"No. I'm her father." Both Sherry and her father spoke at once, but he kept talking. "Get the hell out of my way."

He tried to go around, but Mike blocked him. Nyland seethed, temper visibly rising.

"Do you want to go with him?" Mike asked.

"No. I want him to leave me alone." Sherry tried and failed to pull her arm free.

"I'm your father. You're coming home with me."

Sherry pried at his fingers. "No, I'm not."

"Sir, you'll have to let her go." Mike kept his voice calm, though he could feel his own temper flaring, threatening to burn through his control.

A small crowd was beginning to gather, remaining at a distance, cautious but curious. Mike didn't know yet if it would be to their advantage or not. Probably it was.

"Your daughter is obviously over eighteen." Mike spoke loudly enough for his words to carry. "You can't force her to leave."

"Mind your own damn business." Nyland tried a feint-left-run-right maneuver to get past Mike, but failed to factor Sherry into the move. He jerked her off balance, making her cry out. She was falling to the sidewalk face-first when Mike caught her.

He tried to set her down, but Nyland still had hold of her arm, pulling at her as if she were a wishbone and he'd pull her in two if he had to. Mike kept her wrapped tightly in his arms.

"Do you know who I am?" Nyland trotted out the standard Palm Beach resident line. Every one of them thought their money granted them special treatment. Not in this case. Mike had as much money as Nyland, or more, even if nobody knew it. "I can break you down to nothing."

"Not if you're breaking the law. This is kidnapping. Let her go." Mike leveled his gaze at the sweating man. "Now."

Nyland let go. He looked shocked that he'd obeyed the order and reached for Sherry as if to reclaim his prize, but Mike had her safely behind him now.

"You'd better leave," Mike said. "Go home."

"Not without my daughter."

"I'm not going anywhere with you, Tug." Sherry started to step out to the side, but Mike's raised finger kept her where she was.

"Leave," he repeated. The other man's obstinacy was beginning to seriously annoy him.

Nyland swore. "This isn't the end, Sherry. You're going to marry Greeley."

"No, she isn't." Mike spoke before Sherry could.

"What business is it of yours? Why should you care who she marries?"

Mike had an explanation ready. About how this was the twentieth century and people had rights. About how Sherry worked for him, and he wouldn't let anyone cause trouble at his place of business. About how he would get a restraining order to keep Nyland from coming within a hundred yards of the club. But that wasn't what happened.

What he said was, "Because she's already married to me."

The stunned silence that followed encompassed all three of them. Mike shook his head, trying to clear it. What had he just said? More to the point, why in hell had he said it? When, exactly, had he lost his mind?

At least he recovered it first. To the applause of the crowd that had gathered, most of them from inside his club, he swept Sherry up in his arms since she didn't seem too steady on her feet, and walked away, leaving Tug Nyland sputtering.

He spotted Bruno among the crowd. Great, now gossip would really spread. He headed for the alley. He was not walking back inside the club carrying the woman he'd just announced to the world was his wife. His car was parked out back. Escape sounded like a good plan.

"Mike?" Sherry spoke when he reached the corner of the alley. "You can put me down now. I can walk."

He glanced at her, her face entirely too close to his, shrugged and set her down. When she stumbled, her knees buckling, he picked her back up. Maybe he hadn't found his mind yet after all. He had his body working okay, but his thoughts still seemed to be frozen in shock.

"Mike?" Sherry looped her arms around his neck as he turned. "We're not married."

"I know."

"So why did you tell Tug we were?"

"Hell if I know." He reached his car and tried setting her down again. This time she was a little steadier, maybe because she had the car to hold on to. He unlocked the door and opened it for her. When he got in behind the wheel, she was waiting.

"So what are we going to do now?" she asked.

"I guess we're going to get married." He started the car and pulled out of the lot, trying to force his brain to think where he needed to go in order to do what he needed to do.

"Why? You don't want to marry me."

He sighed. He wasn't up to a lot of conversation right now. He'd just fried his brain with shock.

"Mike?"

But it looked as if he was going to have to make the effort. "I don't want to make a liar out of myself. If we get married, you can't marry the Geek because you're already married to me. That makes what I said true." He hoped that would satisfy her.

Apparently not. "Is that the only reason?" she asked.

"He made me mad," Mike admitted. "He had no business putting his hands on you like that. You were right. He won't give up until he either gets his way, or he understands that what he wants isn't going to happen, no matter what he does."

"Maybe we don't have to actually go through with it. You told him we were married. Maybe that's enough."

Mike shot a glance toward her. She sounded nervous, timid even. That wasn't the Sherry he knew.

"Do you think he won't check the records?" He wasn't about to push her. If she wanted to back out, fine. This was her plan.

She chewed at a thumbnail briefly before hiding her thumb inside her fist. "No. He'd check. He would assume you're lying. He lies so much, he thinks everybody else does, too."

"Then we'll make it fact. No problem."

"Are you sure?" Sherry turned her china-blue gaze on him, and he had to look away.

He couldn't make this personal. She needed his name, his protection, nothing more. He could feel sorry for her, feel protective, but other feelings were not allowed. No possessiveness, no passion and, most especially, no tenderness. This would be hard enough as it was, because he already liked her. It was a steep, slippery slope from there to being in over his head.

"Just so we understand each other," he said in self-defense. "This is strictly business. We'll get married long enough to make your pop back off. Till you get your money. Then it's over. Got it?"

"Gotten." Sherry nodded.

"No kissing. No sex. No running around in just a T-shirt. I don't want anything to complicate this. In fact, it would probably be better if you stayed where you are, at Mom's."

"Okay."

He sent her a suspicious look. She was certainly agreeable. Maybe too agreeable? Then again, she was getting everything she asked for. She hadn't actually said she *wanted* to have sex with him. She just said it would be okay if he wanted it.

He wanted it so badly his teeth ached with the wanting, not to mention every other body part he possessed. But he couldn't have it. Because it would be too damn hard to give it up when this was over. And it would be over. The minute she got her hands on that trust fund of hers. He couldn't forget that the money came first.

"When?" Sherry asked.

"Just as soon as I can get all the ducks lined up." Mike pulled into a parking lot and pulled out his cell phone. There had to be somebody he could call tonight. It wasn't that late.

The next morning near noon, Sherry got out of Mike's car in front of the Palm Beach County courthouse. He had called a judge who was a regular customer and was willing to cut through the red tape with a speed that made her head spin.

"Sherry!" Juliana ran across the sidewalk and threw her arms around her sister in an exuberant hug. "I couldn't believe it when you called me."

"I'm not sure I believe it myself." Sherry let Juliana draw her toward the courthouse entrance, while Mike helped Clara out of the back seat of his car.

"You're getting married!" They had to pause for a

squeal and another hug. "This is so exciting. So…so…*je ne sais quoi*."

"Impulsive?"

"Yes. And spontaneous. Free-spirited. We always wanted to be free spirits, didn't we? Well, now you are one." Juliana looped her arm through Sherry's. "Maybe it will rub off. So spill. Who is he? Where did you meet? When did all this happen?"

"We just decided last night." Sherry felt as if she were wading through a swamp, trying to keep to the more solid ground.

When they had discussed witnesses during the whirlwind wedding preparations, Sherry had asked to invite Juliana. Mike quickly agreed, as long as Juliana was encouraged to believe theirs was a real marriage, so she could help convince Tug to give up on his quest. They had told Clara the truth.

"We met at La Jolie," Sherry said. "When he was working."

"He's a bartender?" Juliana's eyes opened wide in shock.

"He does a little of everything. He manages the place."

Shock melted into a grin. "Won't Tug bust a gut when he finds out what he does?"

Sherry grinned back. "You'll have to take notes and tell me all about it. Come meet him."

"Oh my, my, my." Juliana leaned closer, stretching a little to murmur in Sherry's ear as they neared the others. "There is something to be said for the rugged man of action, isn't there?"

Sherry just smiled. Juliana didn't know how right she was. That kiss, the single kiss he'd given her, had curled not only her toes, but her fingers, her eyelashes and all of her internal organs, as well. She would have thought it had curled her hair, too, but when she looked in the mirror the next day, it had been as straight as always. She could see no external sign that such an earth-shattering, molecule-rearranging kiss had ever occurred.

Every touch, every glance since then had increased the impact, and when he'd carried her in his arms last night, it had been all she could do to keep from kissing that hollow at the base of his throat. If she had, she'd have gone on kissing her way down his body. She didn't know why she was acting this way. She'd never felt these kinds of crazy urges before.

She wasn't a virgin. She'd grown up in Palm Beach, where sex was just another after-school activity. She'd lost her virginity late for this town—at fifteen beside her boyfriend's pool while his parents were away. She'd hoped sex would make him hers, make him love her, but of course it hadn't. At least he'd had a good time. Sherry hadn't, particularly.

She'd had a few other boyfriends since—guys who seemed as if they might be worth the bother of having sex with. None of them were. But with them, she'd never wanted to do any of the things that had been floating through her mind about Micah since that kiss.

Obviously the kiss had not had the same effect on Mike, or he wouldn't have eliminated the possibility of more from this mock marriage they were getting into. Then again, her lame "all right" to sex didn't exactly convey her growing enthusiasm for the idea. That was totally his fault. How could he expect a girl to say anything after she'd been kissed like that?

Quick introductions were made, which included a smile from Mike that made Sherry go weak at the knees, and they formed up for the procession into the courthouse. Clara led the way with Mike's sisters on either side of her, while Mike wheeled the oxygen behind. She hadn't wanted to bring it, but Mike had blackmailed her, threatening not to let her come, to take his sister Nina as his witness to the wedding instead, unless she agreed to bring the oxygen. And use it. The argument had amused Sherry greatly.

Clara dawdled, moving even slower than she usually did. The explanation came when a delivery boy hurried into the courthouse lobby, carrying a long florist's box.

"Here we are." Clara's fluttery sleeves flapped like semaphore flags as she waved her arms to get his attention. "Tip the boy, Micah."

He scowled, reaching into his pocket. The flowers were obviously all Clara's doing. Sherry could tell Mike wanted to complain, but with a glance at Juliana's watching eyes, he held his peace. If they wanted her to believe, flowers would help.

Six cream-colored roses nestled inside the box, each petal edged with deep pink. Their long stems were tied with pink-and-navy ribbons to match Sherry's tired dress. There was even a matching rose for Mike's lapel. Since she hadn't had time to find anything special to wear, the flowers made the event seem a little more special. Which was *not* a good idea.

Despite what they wanted Juliana to believe, this wouldn't be a real marriage. Still, the wedding ceremony itself was real. Sherry supposed that would have to be enough.

The wedding was in the smaller courtroom, the ceremony squeezed in between two divorce hearings. Sherry sometimes thought that marriage and divorce were the primary form of entertainment in Palm Beach. It made her sad to think she would be adding to the statistics; but this make-believe marriage would give her the chance to try again later. In the end she would have the time and space to find—if not true love—at least better-than-average love.

At the moment, *any* love might be nice, as long as she

didn't have to jump through hoops to get it. Whatever love came her way in the future would have to be "as is" love. The kind that loved in spite of everything. She refused to settle for anything less.

Six

The ceremony was soon over, the words all spoken, the vows made. Juliana wanted to treat them all to a late lunch at the Mar-al-Lago—Donald Trump's extravaganza of a private club, where he even lived in his own set of rooms— but Mike insisted they go to a nice restaurant just across the bridge, outside of Palm Beach. Sherry didn't see that it mattered, but apparently Mike did. After lunch, Juliana delivered the suitcase she'd packed for Sherry and headed back to Palm Beach. Then Clara announced that she was ready to collect her things and go home.

"Not yet." Mike opened the back door of his car for her.

"Why not?" Clara glared at him over her oxygen cannula. "You're married now. Sherry's father can't bother her anymore."

"He can still bother her plenty. You bother Nina, don't you? She's been married for years."

"You know what I mean." Clara poked him. "He can't make her marry that other man. The Greek."

"I don't think he's Greek," Sherry murmured. "Prussian, maybe."

Mike ignored her. "But he doesn't know it yet."

"Well, you did tell him…" Sherry didn't know whether she had any right to participate in this family discussion. She was—technically—married to Mike, but it wasn't like it was a real marriage, was it?

"See?" Clara jumped on Sherry's statement. "He knows. I can come home. I am going to come home."

Mike turned on Sherry, his eyes hard. "Do you think he believed me? Do you think it will stop him? You know the man better than I do."

She opened her mouth intending to answer, but Mike stepped closer, right next to her, filling her vision, her senses. He smelled like soap and man in the sun. She couldn't think, forgot everything she meant to say and stood there looking like a landed fish.

"Do you really think my mother will be safe?" He lowered his voice to an intimate caress. "Honestly?"

Sherry shivered, the sun's warmth suddenly not enough. "No," she whispered.

"Then tell her that." Mike backed away, and Florida returned.

"Give it a little more time," Sherry said. "Tug is stubborn. He won't give up until he's convinced beyond any doubt. You don't have to worry about your things. I'll be staying in your—"

"Oh no, you won't." Clara interrupted with a slash of her hand, edging forward till she was in the space Mike had just evacuated. "You are married to my son and you are going to live in his house."

"Mom, we explained—"

She cut Mike off with another wave. "I don't care what

you explained. Marriage is marriage. Besides, how are you
going to convince this Tug person—what kind of name is
Tug anyway? Makes him sound like a boat, not a human
being.''

Sherry laughed, hoping to lighten the atmosphere. ''If
you'd ever seen him under full steam, you'd know that he
looks more like a boat.''

''You can't make him believe you're really married if
you're not living together.'' Clara finished her statement.
''You couldn't possibly expect him to believe it.''

Sherry looked at Mike and found him looking back, his
expression resigned. ''She's right,'' she said.

''I know.'' He took a deep breath and let it out. ''Okay.
We'll move you back to my place. And, Mom, you're going back to Nina's. No arguments.''

Clara deflated, looking sour. ''Oh, fine. No arguments.
But that doesn't mean no grumbling.''

''If you ever stopped grumbling, I'd have to rush you to
the hospital to make sure you were still alive.'' Mike took
her arm and, finally, assisted her into the car.

''I'm not staying here forever, either,'' his mother announced when Mike pulled into his sister's drive. ''Two
days.''

''Two weeks.'' He thought he could make sure Nyland
knew he'd lost in that length of time.

''One.''

''Two.'' He had to hold firm. Mom didn't negotiate. She
battered the other side into capitulation the instant she
found the smallest crack in their armor.

''I'll take it under consideration,'' she said huffily. ''I
love my grandchildren, but truthfully, teenagers are ex-
hausting.''

Sherry opened her door and Clara leaned forward to

touch her shoulder. "Micah can walk me in, dear. I'd like a few minutes for a little mother-son talk."

"I already know about sex, Mom." Mike rolled his eyes.

"You might think you know all about sex, Micah Thomas, but you do not know everything." She latched on to his wrist with an iron grip, not weaker than the one he remembered in childhood, and let him lift her out of the car. The oxygen followed.

Clara pulled the cannula out now and flung it at the tank. Mike let her. It would make the trip up to the front door take twice as long, but she'd done as he'd asked on the wedding expedition, so he wouldn't complain. He would even listen to what she had to say.

"Micah, I want you to promise me that you will do your best with this marriage."

"Mom, it's not like—"

"Don't tell me what it's not. I'll tell you what it *is*. You're married to that girl. Married. You wouldn't have done it if you didn't like her. Maybe even more than like her."

He shook his head. Why didn't she understand? "Okay, maybe I do like her. But that's not enough. I want what you and Dad had. I won't settle for less."

"Do you see me asking you to?"

"Yes."

She made an exasperated noise in the back of her throat. "I'm not telling you to settle. I'm telling you to give it a chance. You'll never find what you want if you don't take any risks. Stop playing it safe. Give Sherry a chance."

"She's from Palm Beach. She grew up there. She has a twenty-million-dollar trust fund she's getting in a few months. You know what those people are like. Selfish to the bone."

"I know what Babs was like—or Bitsy or Buffy or whatever the hell the woman's name was. But she's only one person. They can't all be like that.''

''Only one pers—'' He broke off, shaking his head in wonder. ''Look at Sherry's dad. He's worse than Blair ever thought about being. I can name two dozen people, without even thinking hard, who are *exactly* like that. I know them, Mom. I deal with them every day.''

''Okay, so there's two dozen of them. How many people live in Palm Beach? Ten thousand? That's a lot of lumping Micah, to lump them all in the same pile. What about Sherry's sister? She seemed awfully nice.''

''*Seemed*. You don't *know*.''

''Well, neither do you.'' His mother stopped at the bottom of the step to Nina's wide sunny front deck and glared up at him. He couldn't prevent the little quiver of fear he felt deep inside him at the fire in her eyes.

''Micah Thomas Scott, I swear if you do not stop feeling sorry for yourself and get down off your snobbish high horse and *try* to make this marriage work, not only will I make the rest of your life miserable, I will get your father to come back and help me haunt you.''

He laughed. Big mistake. Mom stabbed her long narrow finger hard into his stomach. He wasn't ready, though he should have been, and it felt as if she'd poked a hole clear through his liver.

''And I'll get Noble to move me back into my apartment this afternoon.'' She followed up her first threat with a more deadly one, one Mike knew she would carry out. His teenaged nephew was a pushover when it came to his grammy.

''Okay, okay. I'll try. But don't blame me when Sherry hightails it out of our lives the minute she gets her money.''

''I most certainly will blame you if I think for one second you pushed her there. I understand why you're keeping quiet about the real state of your finances when you've got thirty million of your own and more rolling in every day, but this pity party of yours has to end, Micah.''

What pity party? Exercising a little caution didn't mean he was feeling sorry for himself. ''I said I'd try, Mom. Okay? What else do you want from me?'' He tried to move her onto the deck, and after some initial resistance finally succeeded.

''I want you to do it,'' she said. ''Not just say it. I know you, Micah. All your life you've said this and said that and then done what you damn well pleased.''

''Don't swear, Mom.''

''Why not? You do it. Promise me, Micah.''

''It doesn't sound right coming out of your mouth. And I promise.''

She turned back at the front door and gave him a hard look.

''I promise,'' he repeated, holding up his right hand.

After another long hard stare, her expression softened and she patted his arm. ''You're a good boy, Micah. Sometimes.''

Mike opened the door and set the oxygen inside, turning escort duty over to his nephew who was waiting patiently.

''Don't forget what you promised.'' She got one last instruction in before the door closed and he turned to walk back to the car and his waiting bride.

His bride.

He had always expected to say those words some day, had even once known who she would be. Or he thought he had. Until she had made it apparent that she wasn't marrying him, just his bank account. A few years had gone down the road since then, years in which he hadn't been looking for a replacement. But that didn't mean he'd spent his time wallowing in self-pity.

Nor did it mean that Sherry was Ms. Right, no matter how much his mom might want her to be. In fact, Mike was ninety-nine-point-nine percent sure she was Ms. Wrong.

He had promised his mother he would try to make this marriage work. That meant fitting Sherry into his lifestyle. Not exactly the sort of lifestyle set by those who'd never had to work for their money. He would immerse her in it, and she would be running scared well before her trust-fund birthday in August.

Sherry Nyland, temporarily Sherry Scott, would never fit into his world, just as he would never fit into hers. Proving it would be easy, and he could keep his promise while he did.

The sun was bright and almost-summer hot when they reached the building where Mike and his mother lived. Sherry deliberately did not think "home," no matter how easy it was. This wasn't her home. Would never be. The silent ride back from Mike's sister's house had made that abundantly clear. And that was the way she wanted it.

She got out of the car without waiting for Mike to open the door. Although he beat her to the door to the lobby, she got to the elevator first and punched the call button. The little competition made her want to smile, but Mike's semiscowl stifled the temptation. What did he really think about this?

When they got off on the eighth floor, two not-quite-teenage girls in neon-bright swimsuits and flowered flip-flops stood waiting for the elevator. As Mike held the elevator door open for them, the skinny blond girl of the pair leaped back toward the corner of the hallway.

"Come on, Mom!" she shouted. "The elevator's here. You are so slow."

"I'm coming, I'm coming. Keep your pants on."

Seconds later, two women in swimsuits and cover-ups rounded the turn. The younger of the two was obviously the blond girl's mother, given her harassed expression, the towels overflowing her beach bag and the tube of sunscreen she held out insistently. "Use it. I'm not listening to you whine about sunburn."

The girl rolled her eyes, but took the sunscreen.

"Well, hello, Michael," the mother said, ogling him up and down, when she noticed Mike standing there.

Sherry took comfort from the fact that the woman obviously did not know him well enough to know his name wasn't Michael. She took no comfort at all, however, from the twinge of jealousy that caused the original comfort.

"Don't you look fabulous," the woman went on. "Where have you been so early, all dressed up?"

The woman took advantage of Mike's kindness in holding the elevator to straighten a lapel on his suit that didn't need straightening. Her daughter rolled her eyes. The other woman hid a smile, while the second girl, plump and dark-haired, looked confused. Sherry tried not to seethe, without much success.

"I got married this morning," he said.

The two women and blond girl stared, mouths dropping open in shock. The other girl still looked confused, but she took over the elevator-door-holding job when asked.

Mike grinned and put his arm around Sherry's waist, pulling her tight against him. She thought he was enjoying this entirely too much. Come to think of it, though, she didn't exactly object to being pressed tight to all those muscles of his.

He indicated first to the older woman, then the younger, then the girls as he introduced them, "Donna, Lanita, Katie—and I don't know you, Miss—"

"Tracy," the door-holder whispered.

"Tracy," he repeated with a smile that made the girl sigh. "Ladies, this is my wife, Sherry Scott. Sherry, these ladies are our neighbors. Donna is in 806, and Lanita and Katie live in 808.''

Sherry smiled and waved, but had time for nothing more. She squeaked as Mike swept her up in his arms and carried her toward the front door of his apartment.

"Talk to you ladies later," he said, and they were inside, the door closing behind them.

Immediately his grin vanished. He deposited her in the middle of the living room and walked into the kitchen without speaking.

Sherry swayed a moment until she found her balance, overwhelmed by the strong arms she could somehow still feel around her, beneath her, holding her up. "What was that?"

"Can't convince your dad unless we convince the neighbors, can we?" he said. "Want a beer?"

"No, thanks." Did that mean carrying her was such a traumatic experience that he needed a drink when it was over? She didn't know. Her head still spun from his rapid-fire mood swings. Only his mood wasn't really swinging. He was just acting.

She followed him into the kitchen and found herself fascinated by the motion of his strong throat as he tipped his head back and drank from a beer can. There, just under his jaw, the faint shadow of his afternoon beard faded into vulnerability and she had to swallow, too. This might be harder than she thought. Especially since Clara had more or less blackmailed them into staying in the same apartment.

"Sure you're not thirsty?" Mike was watching her the way she watched him. He held out his already-sweating can as if offering to share.

"I'll have some ice water." She needed something to cool herself down, though she wasn't sure ice water would do the job.

Sherry got a glass from the cabinet while Mike broke ice from the trays. The water had the typical flat oceanfront taste. Not bottled designer water by any stretch, but it was cold and wet and felt good going down. It took her mind off Mike's throat—and the places on it perfect for kissing.

She set the glass on the counter. "I guess I'd better go get my suitcase."

"No." He drank again.

Sherry didn't notice his neck this time. She was too busy glaring at him. "No? What do you mean, no?"

"Just what I said. No." He leaned against the kitchen counter, watching her without expression, but Sherry had no doubt something was going on behind that bland exterior. Probably lots of somethings. She wished she knew what they were.

"Does that mean you're going out to get it for me?"

"No."

Now she was annoyed. What happened to the nice guy? Not that he was so nice to start with. Or was this what always happened after the wedding? The nice guy turned into the tyrant. "Why not? I want to change clothes."

"Sorry. But nobody's going back downstairs for at least an hour." Mike finished the beer and tossed the can at the swing-topped trash can across the room. It hit the lid and bounced off. "Two hours would be better," he said as he strolled over to pick up his bride.

"Why?" Sherry did not understand.

He sighed. "Because Donna and Lanita are out at the pool with the girls. You have to walk by the pool to get to the garage. And we're newlyweds. Remember?"

He waggled his hand at her so that light glinted off the plain gold band. Clara had provided the rings when they realized they would need the stage props. Mike wore his father's wedding ring, Sherry wore Clara's. She'd argued against using them—the sentimental value of the rings made her uncomfortable. But she hadn't been able to let herself agree to new ones. She didn't want Mike spending his money on her, and she didn't have enough to contribute her share.

"I don't think you should go over to Mom's to get anything, either. They could have left something and come back."

"I remember. We're newlyweds." Sherry ran her thumb across the inside surface of the matching band on her hand. "So what?"

"Are you sure you grew up in Palm Beach?" Mike's forehead creased as he studied her, as if she presented a puzzle he couldn't solve. "Think, Sherry. We just got married. I carried you over the threshold. What are the neighbors going to assume we're doing?"

Heat rushed to her face as she finally put the pieces together. The neighbors would expect them to be involved in hot, sweaty, tempestuous sex right about now. "Oh."

Sherry felt totally stupid. Especially since the idea now swelled up in her mind and took up all the space that normal thoughts usually occupied. She really, truly wished she hadn't seen Mike in nothing but a bath towel. It hadn't left much to the imagination, and her imagination had been working overtime lately. She knew what he had hidden under that shoulder-enhancing jacket and wilted white shirt, and she wanted to see it again.

See it? She wanted to touch.

Which was probably why she hadn't caught on to Mike's explanation of why they were trapped in the house. She was focusing too hard on being angry with him for all those blunt-force *no*s of his, so she wouldn't think about that soft, vulnerable spot just under his jaw begging for a kiss. And now he thought she was ignorant about sex as well as indifferent to it.

"I'm going to change. It's too hot to stay in this coat."

Mike slid out of his suit jacket and headed out of the kitchen. "I can probably find you some shorts and a T-shirt if you want."

"That would be nice, thanks." Sherry took her ice water with her as she wandered back into the living room. "What are we going to do for the next two hours?" She raised her voice so he could hear her through his closed bedroom door. "Vegetate?"

Mike didn't deign to respond. She strolled around the room, inspecting the shelves of videos and music discs collected for the state-of-the-art entertainment system he'd assembled piece by piece. She assumed he'd gathered the components that way, since no three pieces bore the same brand name, except for five of the eight speakers. She thought Clara could listen to his music from next door if he turned it up higher than dead quiet. Heck, Donna and Lanita could probably hear it by the pool.

"We could watch a video," Sherry called, running her finger across the titles that ran the gamut from action-adventure all the way to action-thriller, with a few sophomoric comedies thrown in. "Is there a particular shoot-'em-up, blow-'em-up movie you prefer?"

"Suit yourself. I plan to." Mike tossed two gray somethings at her.

One landed on her shoulder, the other on the floor at her feet. When she investigated, they proved to be shorts and a T-shirt, just as he'd offered.

"Thanks," she began, before she looked up and the rest of her words stuck in her throat.

She had seen him, before, wearing even less than the cutoff T-shirt with ripped-out sleeves and the knit shorts he had on now. Her short-term memory had to be slipping. That was the only explanation. Though she knew she hadn't noticed the tattoo, which was right where he said it was, she did not remember that washboard stomach or the

corded thighs. She did remember that little trail of hair
leading down from his navel.

Sherry squeezed her eyes shut and took a deep breath.
When she opened them, he was gone. Back to his bedroom,
she decided, from the rustling-around noises. But it didn't
really matter where. The man was temptation in bare feet.

With a sigh she went into the other bedroom to change.

Mike straddled the weight bench in his bedroom and sat
down. It wasn't anything fancy, unlike the ones in the
weight room downstairs, but it was enough to help keep
him in shape and he didn't have to leave home. He ducked
his head under the bar as he lay back for some bench press.
The weight was light, since he didn't have a spotter. He
wished he could pile it on. He needed to work hard, to
wear himself out and sweat the woman out of his pores.
The way she'd crawled under his skin, he figured it was
the only way he could get her out again. He did not need
this grief.

He listened over the hum of the air conditioner for her
bedroom door to open, for the TV to click on, as he pushed
his first set of lifts to double the usual number of reps. He
smelled her first, the heady fragrance of woman mixed with
some expensive perfume. Then he saw her watching from
the doorway.

His T-shirt had never looked so good. The faded USMC
stenciled across the front of the well-washed fabric followed every little rise and fall of his new wife's breasts,
making her braless state abundantly clear. She'd knotted
the shirt at her waist and tied a big looping bow in the
drawstring of the shorts to hold them up. Her panty line
showed through the knit shorts. She wore bikinis with wide
elastic. He could see both edges of the elastic where his
shorts draped lovingly over her hips.

Mike never slowed the rhythm of his lifts as he watched

her watch him. He should stop. Tell her to leave. Close his eyes the way she'd closed hers, as if it offended her to look at him in his workout gear.

It offended him to see her now, to see how she watched him, her eyes following the bar down and back up, skimming over him as if he were a pet she could play with for a while then dump out in the swamp for alligator bait when she got through with him. How would that look change if she knew the truth?

He lifted the bar high and settled it in its cradle, then sat up. "Like what you see?"

One of her shoulders lifted a tiny space, then dropped in a careless shrug. "Yes." She paused briefly. "But then, I don't imagine that's any surprise to you."

He allowed himself a brief, bitter laugh. He'd never had any doubt that his looks or his money would pass muster. It was his class that usually got called into question. "No beating around the bush with you, is there, Sherry?"

"I've given it up. You never get anywhere that way."

Mike picked up a small weight and fitted it over the end of the bar. He would add five pounds for the next set of repetitions. He fussed with the weights and the clamps, waiting for her to get bored and go away. She didn't. Finally, he asked, "Was there something you wanted?"

"Is this going to get us in trouble at work? Us getting married?"

"There's no written policy." He gave up waiting—she apparently had no intention of leaving—and lay back down to start his next set. "Nobody's going to say anything."

Sherry came farther into the room, to the foot of the bench. "Are you sure? What about the owner?"

"Yes, I'm sure. The owner doesn't care." Which was a lie. He cared in ways he didn't want to think about.

"How can you be positive?"

"I'm sure, okay?" He'd had enough of this conversation. Why wouldn't she just go away? "Give it a rest, will you, please? It's not any of your business, anyway."

Mike concentrated on his form, keeping the bar balanced neither too far forward or too far back, holding his arms at the exact angle to do himself the most good. She still came seeping through all his cracks and crannies, impossible to ignore.

"I guess not. How can anything about you be any of my business? After all, I'm just your wife."

His temper sparked high. He tossed the heavy bar back into its cradle and leaped to his feet. "Only on paper."

Still straddling the bench, feet spread wide, he bent to put himself nose-to-nose with her. "Got that?" He had to be sure she understood. "Maybe you carried real roses, but this is a paper marriage, and you are a paper wife."

She didn't smell like paper, though. She didn't look like paper, either, all round and sleek and satin soft, with golden skin and pink lips and a little rosy tongue that sang a silent siren's call just by making a slow trip from one corner of her mouth to the other.

Seven

Mike was kissing her before he knew he'd moved, his tongue following the call of hers back into her mouth. She tasted sweet, cool from the water she'd been drinking, but she warmed quickly to his caress. Her hands slipped behind his neck as he pulled her close, easing forward until she nestled in the cradle of his widespread thighs. He filled his hands with her bottom, squeezing, shaping, pressing her tight against his arousal.

He tilted his head the other way, taking the kiss deeper. His knees bent until he was her height, until his erection nudged her mound, told her where he wanted to be. She gasped at the intimate touch, and Mike's brain snapped back where it belonged from the other end of his body.

He stumbled back a few steps and sat down on the bench with a thump, somehow not cracking his head against the weight bar.

Sherry didn't seem any steadier. "What was that?" she rasped out. "A paper kiss?"

Mike wanted to hide his face in his hands, but confined himself to drawing a shaky hand across his mouth. Not to wipe away the kiss—he was sure that kiss was branded on his soul—but in hopes of recovering a little composure.

"'Cause I have to tell you, sweetheart," Sherry went on, her voice a little clearer, "that sure didn't feel like paper. It didn't feel like 'no kissing' or 'no sex,' either. So if you want to enforce your ban, you're going to have to do a whale of a lot better than that."

She backed away till she reached the doorway, then turned and fled the room. Mike scrambled to follow. But what could he say? She was right. He would have to do better.

"Look," he said from the opening to the kitchen, where she was busy refilling her water glass. "Sex isn't a game to play for lack of anything better to do. It should mean something more than just a way to get some feel-good exercise. To *both* of the people involved."

"Why did you kiss me, then?" Sherry turned off the faucet but stayed where she was, staring at the sink.

"Hell if I know." Frustrated, Mike ran both hands back over his hair. "I think my brain dissolved."

She stifled a snicker, badly. Most of it escaped. "How much more?"

"How much more what?" He must not have all his brain cells reconstituted yet, because now he was confused.

"How much more should it mean? Sex…to the people involved…?" Sherry turned and looked at him.

He frowned. "What do you mean?"

"Is it enough to like each other, or do you have to be all the way in love? Obviously, being married isn't enough. So what is?" She bit her lip, reminding Mike that his body still wanted what he wouldn't let it have.

"What does it matter? It isn't going to happen." He wouldn't let his teeth grind together, either.

"Okay, fine. But I still want to know. Hypothetically speaking, if you insist. How much more? In love?"

"It's not something I can put a tape measure to."

"Why not? You're the one making up all these rules. I just want to know what they are."

Mike threw up his hands. Why did she think he had all the answers? "All right. Yes. In love."

"So if people just like each other, sex is out."

"Sure." He agreed for the sake of agreeing.

"What if they like each other a whole lot, but they're not sure if it's love? What if having sex would help them figure out if they love each other? Wouldn't that be all right?"

"Yeah. Why not?"

She was pacing now, from refrigerator to sink, thinking out loud. "But what if they just got swept up in the moment? Carried away by passion?"

"Sherry." Mike was pretty sure that if she didn't stop talking about it, sex would be taking place in the kitchen in the next two minutes. "Leave it alone."

He turned and walked away. Not back to his weight bench. He didn't know if he'd be able to bench press anything again without getting a hard-on. Maybe the living room would be safe.

"So I guess this means you just like me a little bit, right?" Sherry followed him, perching on the arm of a chair.

Mike rummaged through his shelves for a movie. Something safe. Something with a high body count, none of them naked. "I like you fine," he mumbled.

"But not enough for sex."

"Sherry." He put a warning in his voice. "Enough."

"It's okay. It doesn't hurt my feelings. I'm used to people not liking me. Bebe doesn't like me much."

"Who's Bebe?" Mike asked before he could stop himself.

"My stepmother. Remember? She thinks I'm prettier than Juliana. I'm not. Juliana's pretty in a different way. But that's what Bebe thinks, so she hates me."

"I don't hate you." He switched on the TV, giving up on the idea of a movie. Sports would do.

"You don't like me much, either."

He rolled his eyes. "Will you stop? I like you plenty."

"Just not enough to have sex with me."

If he strangled her, they would call it justifiable. "It's not *me* liking *you* that's the problem. It's the other way round."

"I like you. A lot."

"Today."

"I'll like you tomorrow, too."

He did not want to talk about this, but he couldn't stop himself. He was caught in an undertow and it was about to drag him far out to sea. "What about after that? What about when your money comes in? You won't be able to say goodbye fast enough."

That shut her up. For a minute or two.

"You don't know that." She actually sounded as if her feelings were hurt. But that was impossible.

"Sure I do."

"How? How can you possibly know—"

"You're from Palm Beach, babe. You're one of them. And I'm not." Not deep down. Not really. He had enough money to be one, but he didn't care about the right things. Mike sank into one of the cushy club chairs and put the remote through its paces.

"I'm not her, Micah." Sherry's voice came softly, floating just louder than the TV, creeping inside him.

"Her who?"

"Whoever made you feel this way. Whoever played

games with your heart and kicked it aside when she was done. The one from Palm Beach.''

''Don't kid yourself, babe. You're just like her.'' He found a baseball game and slumped lower, till his head rested on the back of the chair. He was lying, of course.

Sherry was different. She'd refused to marry Mr. Moneybags Greeley. Lots of people with fewer advantages than she'd grown up with would turn their noses up at the job he'd given her. Sherry hadn't. She worked hard at it. All of that didn't mean much, though, in light of the trust fund waiting at the end of the summer. He had to make sure she saw the problems, without ever discovering the truth.

''Get me a beer, will ya?'' He clicked over to the fishing show during the commercial. ''Since you're up.''

The silver can came whistling through the air and smacked him in the head. He should have ducked.

They tiptoed around each other for the next few days. Mike took some time off to make things look good, in case Tug investigated, but the close quarters didn't improve things between them. Sherry felt guilty every time she saw the bruise on Mike's forehead where she'd thrown the beer can at him. She'd intended to hit him, just not in the head. She could have killed him.

Then again, probably not. Hard as his head was, she thought a sledgehammer would barely dent it. She'd never known anyone so thick-headed stubborn. Tug took stubborn to a high art, but he was an amateur compared to Sherry's temporary husband.

On Monday Mike had business to take care of off the island. Sherry talked him out of insisting she come with him. She didn't want to trail after him like some idiot who couldn't tie her own shoes, nor did she want to sit in the car and wait. But sitting in the apartment wasn't much more exciting.

After several hours of twiddling her thumbs, flipping through a thousand television channels that had nothing on, cleaning out the refrigerator, eating the rest of a bottle of olives, half a jar of peanut butter and way too many crackers, followed by more thumb twiddling, Sherry couldn't stand it anymore. She grabbed a towel and headed for the beach.

Mike's T-shirt and shorts were about to be introduced to sea water. If Tug showed up—well, Mike would just have to save the princess from the dragon. She was certain he'd rather that than have his apartment upended by a crazed woman sent over the edge by boredom.

Sherry didn't do much more than get wet. She knew better than to actually swim alone. Mostly she sat under a palm tree and watched seagulls fight over scraps of food. The sun and the waves and the breeze gradually soothed away her restlessness and she headed back to the apartment.

When she walked in the door, Clara was waiting.

An hour later Sherry was almost ready for work, hunting her wandering shoes, when Mike walked in the door. He looked way too good in yet another of his fabulous suits, this one black. He wore it with a silvery shirt that matched his eyes.

"How'd it go?" she asked, locating the missing sandals under the edge of the coffee table. She sat down in one of the cushy arm chairs to drag them out.

Mike went still a moment before opening the refrigerator to pull out a drink. "Don't try to play Ozzie and Harriet."

"We can't even talk?" Sherry was getting tired of all Mike's rules.

"We can talk. Just leave off the 'how was your day,' 'honey, I'm home' stuff."

"Okay. Fine." She'd rather throw another beer can at his head. Maybe this time it would knock some sense into him. She stuck her foot in a shoe. "Conversation. Your mother has moved back home. She wants to know why we're not having sex."

Mike froze, the can he was drinking from tipped high. Then he started to cough. Sherry put on her other shoe as she waited for him to recover.

"You told her that?" he croaked between coughs.

"No, I did not." Maybe she'd get one of those super-size cans to whack him with. "I didn't have to. She knew."

"What, exactly, did she say?" He sounded almost normal now.

"Exactly? She said, 'Why aren't you and Mike sleeping together?'"

"What did you say?"

"I said—I didn't know what to say—so I said, 'We are.' And she said, 'Liar.' And I said, 'How do you know?' And she said—"

"Wait." Mike stopped her. "How did you say it? Did you say it like, 'How do *you* know?' or like, 'How do you *know?*'"

"What difference does it make?"

"One way you're saying 'None of your business' and the other way you're saying 'Caught me.' So how did you say it?"

"How should I know?" Sherry couldn't believe this conversation. The man was certifiable. Besides, she wasn't about to admit the truth.

"You told her," Mike said.

"She tricked me!"

"She's like that."

"So are you. You tricked me just now, you sneak. But I expect it of you. You're a man. She's a little old lady. A sneaky, little old lady."

"Who taught me everything I know."

Sherry sighed and pulled one of the decorative pillows

into her lap, carefully combing the tangled fringe straight.
"So what do we do now?"

"Nothing."

"What about your mother?"

He sighed. "She'll give me a lot of grief. I won't pay
her any attention. Things will go on like they are."

"She told me to seduce you." Sherry didn't understand
that. "Do you think she meant it?"

"Probably. Are you going to do it?"

"Do you want me to?"

"Do you want to?"

"Can you say anything without turning it into a question?" Now the conversation was getting silly.

"I don't know, can I?" He turned it back on her once
more with a wicked grin.

Sherry laughed and tossed the pillow at him, which he
caught and threw back at her.

"You know," he said. "For somebody who got all up-
tight over whacking me on the arm a few short days ago,
you sure have turned violent all of a sudden. I went to the
club for a minute this afternoon and had to tell everybody
that my wife coldcocked me with a beer can. I'm a victim
of domestic violence."

"You told them?" Her stomach did a funny little dance.

"I told them the truth. Mostly. You were tossing me a
beer and missed. Don't worry about it."

"No, I mean, you told them we were married?" It made
it seem more real that he'd told their co-workers.

"They already knew. Bruno followed me outside the
night your dad came to the club. He heard me. When I
said…what I said. That's the idea, isn't it? For people to
know we're married, so your dad will leave you alone."

"Okay, yes, but—" Why did she feel so uncomfortable?

"I went ahead and put you on my insurance, just in case,
but I didn't make any other changes, if that's what you're

worried about. You don't mind, do you? I just want to be sure somebody's close by to make sure Mom gets the treatment she needs if I'm away. Putting you as my next of kin will do that.''

He'd named her next of kin?

Sherry had to take a deep breath. Maybe his accusations did have cause. Maybe she had been seeing all of this, their marriage and everything associated with it, as a game. As playing make-believe, something she could put back in the box like dress-up clothes when it was over and forget about. Mike would be hard to forget, but she thought she could do it. It wasn't as if she was in love with him or anything.

But it was real. Maybe not all the way real, given their sleeping arrangements, but a lot more so than she had let herself realize. When a man started talking about next of kin and life-or-death situations, things couldn't get much more real than that.

"I'm going to go clean up before we head in for work," he said, throwing away his empty can.

Sherry met him halfway across the living room and threw her arms around his neck.

Mike set his hands on her waist. "What's going on?" He sounded puzzled.

She was, too. She didn't know why she'd done it. Sherry turned and rushed into her bedroom before she could embarrass herself anymore and shut the door. He didn't have to know how much she liked him.

Two days later Mike was at his mom's, cooking dinner before work. He did it whenever he could because he liked knowing she had eaten, knowing what she'd eaten and knowing she wouldn't be sneaking around cooking things.

The elevator rattled as it arrived on their floor, loud enough to be heard over his own rattling around in the kitchen. He'd have to call someone and get it worked on.

It shouldn't make that much noise. Mike paused to listen, trying to tell who might be getting off. Sherry had taken the car this afternoon to "run errands," but she ought to be back. It would be time to head into work soon.

He hadn't insisted on going with her today, because she swore she'd be safe, and he knew she was too afraid of her father to say so if it weren't true. Since Mike hadn't a clue where she planned to go, he figured Nyland wouldn't, either. She wasn't back, but he wasn't worried. Not exactly.

They'd been getting hang-up phone calls over the past few days, both at Mom's and at his place. He suspected her father, but hadn't gotten round to getting the phone company to put a trace on the line. They didn't come often enough to be harassing, and no one ever spoke, but they made him uneasy, and they had Sherry jumping at shadows. She didn't need more grief from the man.

"Sherry's back," his mom said from her perch on a kitchen chair. She liked to supervise his cooking, even though it had been many years since he set the oven on fire trying to bake one giant chocolate-chip cookie. It hadn't occurred to him then that the dough would expand and drip off the sides of the cookie sheet.

"How do you know?" He tasted the pasta sauce and added more oregano.

"Because if it was Donna or Lanita and Katie, they'd have gone the other way. Your apartment is the only one past mine."

"Is that how you spy on me?"

She ignored him. "Aren't you going to go get her? Tell her where you are?"

"She's a smart girl." He lifted the lid of the other pot to see if the water was boiling yet. "When she sees I'm not over there, she'll figure it out."

"Aren't you going to go kiss her hello?" His mother sounded annoyed.

Mike hid his grin. "With my mother watching?" He gave a fake shudder. "Heavens, no."

"Come over here so I can stick you with this fork." She waved the utensil menacingly.

"I'm not that stupid." He had to laugh. She was half bark, and half bite. Trouble was, he could never tell which half he would get.

The front door burst open and slammed shut again hard enough to rattle the family pictures in the living room. Sherry had arrived.

"Guess what?" She dropped a small pile of shopping bags near the door, bounded into the kitchen and threw her arms around Clara hard enough to half knock her out of the chair before hugging her gently.

She bounced over to Mike, and before he knew what hit him, she threw her arms around his neck and planted a big kiss right on his mouth. Then she was gone. Long before he could recover from the brain explosion caused by the feel of her curves pushed hard against him, the scent of woman overwhelming tomato and basil, the taste of mint and woman left behind on his lips. He wanted her back, where he could catch and hold on, taste more, smell more. Feel more.

"Guess what?" she said, yet one more time.

"I don't know. What?" Mike tucked his hands in his front pockets to keep from reaching out for her.

"I'm back." Her wide grin never faded. "And I had a wonderful time, all by myself without a bodyguard."

She swooped back in for another fierce hug, one more quick kiss, and, damn it, his hands were stuck in his pockets. He couldn't get them out fast enough to capture her before she flitted away to kiss his mother's cheek.

"Congratulations." His mom apparently understood what was going on.

A girl thing, Mike guessed. He didn't know if that was a good or a bad thing.

"Thank you." Sherry twirled in a circle, her skirt flaring out slightly before she collapsed in the chair across from his mother.

"Where did you go?" Mike asked. "What did you do?" He assumed she hadn't seen Nyland given the mood she was in.

The lid to the pasta pot rattled, telling him the water boiled. He gave it only half his attention as he poured in the corkscrew shapes, while watching Sherry.

She waved a hand languidly through the air. "Oh, you know. Places. Stores. The mall. I went to one of those mega-hyper-super-discount stores for the very first time in my life."

"What did you think?" Clara perked up a little. She loved those stores. "What did you buy?"

"Absolutely nothing." Sherry laughed as she gave a mock shudder. "By the time I followed the trail of bread-crumbs back to the door again, after being lost for hours and hours, I was too intimidated to even think about buying anything. Besides, what do you do with a fifty-pound sack of rice or five pounds of chili powder?"

Mike took two steps to the pantry and opened it to dis-play huge packages of rice, pasta, chips, pickles and what-ever else had caught his mother's eye. "I've been trying to figure that out."

Sherry's eyes went wide, then she burst out laughing. "Good thing I was intimidated, huh?"

"Good thing." Mike stared at her, frowning. "Some-thing's different. You look different somehow. What is it?"

She turned her gaze on him, eyebrows rising in question. "You can't tell?"

His eyes narrowed, skimmed over her, trying to pinpoint the change. New dress, sunny-yellow color, but she'd worn it when she left, so it was probably from the bottomless suitcase her sister had packed. Same great legs, same sleek curves, same smile, same eyes, same nose, same golden hair.

"You cut your hair!" He couldn't keep the triumph from his voice. He'd figured it out on his own.

Sherry laughed and shook her head, the short, ear-length locks tumbling all directions. "I can't believe you didn't notice. It doesn't even reach my chin."

"You have to forgive him, dear." Clara reached across the table and patted Sherry's hand. "He's a man. You can't kiss him like that and expect him to comprehend more than one thing at a time."

"Like that?" Sherry gave him a sideways look. "But that was scarcely a kiss at all."

That was the truth. Two scarcely-a-kisses didn't add up to even one real kiss. Not that Mike wanted one. Or rather, not that he wanted one with his mother looking on, smiling one of her patented "told you" smiles. He couldn't have one, anyway. Not the kind of kiss he wanted.

There. He admitted it. He wanted to kiss his wife. Wanted a hell of a lot more than kisses, truth be told. But he couldn't have it. Because if he ever got what he wanted, everything would change, and that would lead straight to disaster, deep ocean and high winds driving him under till he never came up again.

"Who's ready to eat?" Mike reached for the strainer to drain the pasta.

Immediately Sherry got up and went to the sink to wash her hands, then proceeded to fix drinks for supper.

"So?" she said.

"So, what?" Mike frowned at her. What did she want?

"So, what do you think about my haircut?"

Her tone of voice made it clear this wasn't the first time she'd asked. He needed to pay more attention to the conversation and less—a lot less—to kisses, hypothetical or otherwise.

"I like it," he said, pouring the noodles into a serving bowl. He picked up the pan with the meatballs and rationed his mom's share onto her plate. She could have three. No more.

"Micah Scott, you haven't even looked at it. How can you possibly know if you like it or not?"

He shrugged. "Because it's your hair." He'd like it however it was cut, because it was attached to her. How could it look anything but good? He put the rest of the sauce and meatballs in a bowl and set them on the table.

"Mike." Sherry poked him lightly in the arm. "Look first, okay? I want an honest opinion."

He looked, against his better judgment.

Her hair tumbled about her face as if she just got out of bed. It made her look both younger, more vulnerable somehow, and at the same time older, more mature. She ducked her head, as if uncomfortable under his scrutiny. The action exposed her pale nape, no longer protected from the sun— or his eyes—by the long veil of hair.

That curve of smooth bare skin at the back of her neck made him want to howl. Her new haircut transformed her into some kind of sultry, seductive sex goddess. How in the hell was he supposed to resist that?

He swallowed, hard, his mouth suddenly dry. "Oh, yeah. I like it just fine." His voice came out rough edged, raspy.

His mother cackled from her seat at the table, seeing everything he didn't want her to see.

"Honestly?" Sherry sounded as if she wanted to believe him, but couldn't quite. "It's not too short?"

"It looks good. Great, in fact." He slapped a serving spoon down beside the pasta. "Trust me. Now sit down and eat."

Sherry sat and surveyed the table. "Don't you usually serve meatballs with spaghetti, rather than rotini?"

"We were out." He served her plate with pasta. "Eat."

After dinner Sherry hurried through the dishes, despite the way Clara kept insisting she could do them and they needed to hurry off to work. Sherry didn't want Mike accusing her of failing to keep up her end of things. When everything was spotless, Clara almost pushed them out the door. It might have hurt Sherry's feelings if she weren't halfway sure Clara was playing matchmaker again. Maybe she thought they'd be overwhelmed by passion while they were changing for work. They were halfway down the hall when Clara's front door opened again.

"Oh, wait," she called. "Come back. I forgot something."

"What?" Mike stopped walking, but didn't turn back. Sherry followed his lead. He knew his mother's sneaky ways.

"Something came for you today, Sherry. It was in my mailbox, addressed to you." Clara started after them, and Mike hurried back to take her arm.

"What is it?" He took the thick square envelope from his mother and glanced at it curiously before handing it to Sherry.

"Well, I don't know," Clara said. "I don't go around opening other people's mail."

Mike snorted in disbelief.

Clara ignored him. "It looks like a wedding invitation." She pointed at the postmark. "It's local. Palm Beach. You know anybody getting married?"

Sherry stared at the envelope a moment longer, her heart pounding. "It does, doesn't it?" Surely Tug wouldn't send invitations to a wedding that wouldn't happen. Couldn't. She was already married. To Mike.

Nobody ever sent an invitation to the bride. It couldn't be what she was afraid it was.

She opened it and pulled out the inside envelope, her hands shaking. She had to pause and wipe her palms on her skirt before removing the card inside.

"What is it?" Mike asked again.

Sherry read the message a second time trying to comprehend.

"Well?" Clara demanded. "Is it a wedding invitation?"

"Close." Sherry blinked back sudden, surprising tears. "It's an invitation to a wedding reception. My baby sister's getting married. Apparently, I'm still in disgrace, since I'm not invited to the wedding."

That hurt. But at least Juliana had made sure she got invited to the reception.

"Too bad I won't be going." She shoved the invitation back into the envelope. She didn't dare go. Confronting Tug on his own turf wasn't even something she wanted to think about.

"I think you should go." Mike took the invitation from her still-shaking fingers. "I think *we* should go. Together."

"I don't think so," Sherry said. "The reception's at the house. I don't want to go back there."

A soft click barely registered in Sherry's hearing. Part of her noticed Clara wasn't there anymore and realized the click was the door closing; but most of Sherry focused on Mike.

"I won't let you out of my sight." Mike read the invitation for himself. "It's the perfect opportunity to prove to your father—and everyone else—that we're married and he can't marry you off to some geek with money."

A shudder ran through her at the memory of Tug's grip on her arm as he marched her out of the club. She never wanted to feel so helpless again. "I really don't want to—"

"Don't want to show your sister how happy you are for

her? Don't want to take the chance to convince your father?''

"We might not."

"Then you'll still be no worse off than before. But we might pull it off, and then you'll have him off your back.''

Sherry bit her lip, uncertainty eating at her. "I'm afraid,'' she said, something she could admit only to him.

"I know." He touched her shoulder. "But it'll be okay. Promise."

She wanted to step into his arms, take the reassurance he offered. How long would the offer be good? She couldn't start to depend on him. One day, not too far off, she would have only herself to lean on. But his promises were so tempting.

"How can you be so sure?" she whispered.

"Because I'll be right there with you. I'll never let anyone hurt you. *Never.*"

Eight

Mike's gray eyes blazed with the force of his words, lightning behind storm clouds. Sherry shivered before their fierce power, wanting to believe him, believe in his promises. But she had wanted to believe so many times before, and every time—every single, sorry, stinking time—the promises had been no more than sand castles on the beach, forgotten as high tide washed them away.

If only one person in her life had forgotten their promises, Sherry might be able to believe that Mike could be trusted…because he was different, heart and soul different. But his difference didn't matter. The problem was with Sherry.

She was invisible. Forgettable. Clearly unimportant. Otherwise, why would so many promises, made to her by so many people, have been broken?

He brushed back her short, unruly hair and let his fingers trail along her cheek. "Trust me."

How could she? She wasn't important to him. He'd made that abundantly clear. How long before he forgot about her in the excitement of the party?

"Have I ever let you down?" His eyes flashed lightning again.

She shook her head. "Not so far. But it's barely been a week."

He gripped her shoulders tight, arms taut as if he held himself in firm control. "What do I have to do to convince you that I'm not like all those jerks you know here in Palm Beach?"

"Oh, I know you're different, Mike. But we both know that I'm not." Sherry broke free and hurried to his front door. She had to get away, hide her exposed weakness before anyone saw it and used it to rip her wide open.

"Sherry, wait." Mike caught her arm as she reached the door and spun her around. "That's not true. You're not like them. I didn't want to admit it, okay? But you're—" He faltered, hunting words. "You," he said helplessly. "You're you."

She frowned. "What does that mean?"

"If I knew, I'd have said that instead. I…you—" Again his fingers traced along the side of her face, brushing through her new short hair. "Let me take care of you, please? Can you trust me to do that?"

"Why?" It seemed to matter a great deal to him, and she did not understand it.

"Because you're my wife."

A smile forced its way to her lips. "For a minute I was afraid you were going to do that 'you're you' bit again. But it's not real. I'm just your paper wife."

"Real enough." His fingers slid back into her hair and he cupped her cheek in his palm. "To the world you're my wife. What kind of man would I be if I let anything happen to you?"

Ah. Now she had it. Pride was involved. That masculine code that men understood and women never quite got.

"Will you go to your sister's party with me?" He stroked his thumb along her cheekbone, his hand warming her cheek. She suppressed a shudder in reaction. "Will you trust me to look after you?"

His touch created a slow-rising sensual haze that was beginning to fog her brain, but Sherry retained enough presence of mind to nod her head. She could trust him to do what he said, because it wasn't about her. It was about his image as a man.

"Good," he murmured as his head lowered and his lips grazed across hers.

She leaned into the teasing kiss, needing more. His hand, the one not tipping her face up toward his, slid to her waist, warm and heavy. He returned his mouth to hers, open now, and his tongue traced the seam of her lips. Sherry opened to him, helpless to resist his sensual entreaty. He slid inside, wiping away all knowledge of anything but Micah Scott.

He stroked the inner contours of her mouth, and she sank deeper into the haze of rising passion as she answered his every caress with one of her own. Oh, she needed this. She knew he didn't mean anything by it, knew the kisses would go nowhere, given his "sex should mean something" speech. But while he kissed her, she could pretend for just a little space of time that she meant something to somebody.

"Whoa! Hey, go home for that." Only after the woman spoke did Sherry hear the rattle of the elevator as it departed. "We can't even come up the elevator without having to hide Katie's eyes, just in case you two are out in the hall."

Sherry broke the kiss, but Mike wouldn't let her pull away. He tucked her head into his shoulder, holding her close. She understood why, the instant their bodies touched.

Mike was fully, magnificently aroused. A twelve-year-old girl didn't need to see that. Neither did her mother or anyone else.

"Just a kiss, Donna," Mike said. "It won't hurt her to see a kiss. Besides, Katie's not with you."

The older woman, the widow, had seen their kiss, not the divorcee. Sherry's knees wilted in relief. Of course, they were pretty wilted to begin with.

"Hon, that was *not* just a kiss. That was foreplay. And I do not need any reminders of what I'm missing. Take it inside, mister."

With a laugh Mike walked Sherry the few paces to his front door, holding her in place. Every step made her more aware of just how aroused he was, and as her awareness increased, so did her longing to know what it would be like to make love with this man. His reasons for refusing made her want it all the more.

Her blood raced with the pounding of her heart, echoing the beat sounding through the hard wall of his chest. He obviously desired her. Could he want her enough to get past his dislike? Could she have a few more minutes of this make-believe love?

Then he closed the front door and walked away. "I need a shower," he said as he vanished into his bedroom.

Sherry took a deep breath and sank into a chair before her knees gave way. So nothing would happen tonight. But that didn't mean nothing would happen tomorrow. Or the next night. She had months. As long as she didn't fool herself into thinking she'd have forever, she'd be fine.

She knew better than to think he could fall in love with her. But she was so tired of having nothing at all.

Juliana called the next Tuesday night. She was marrying Kurt Collier at three-thirty on Wednesday afternoon, not

Friday before the party. Would Mike and Sherry be their witnesses?

"Absolutely. But isn't this a little sudden?" Sherry didn't know whether her concern was for her sister or herself. No matter when Juliana married, the reception would still go on. Sherry had nervous megrims at the thought of going back in that house.

"Who are you to be talking about sudden?" Juliana laughed. "We were getting married anyway. We're just moving it up a few days."

"I take it you're smitten, then."

Juliana actually giggled. Sherry didn't think she'd ever heard her sister giggle. At least not in the last few years.

"I am not smitten, Sher. I'm smashed flat. I know it won't last, but while it does, I intend to enjoy every minute."

"What about Kurt? Is he smitten?"

"I...don't know." Juliana's uncertainty came through loud and clear. "How can you tell?"

"Does he at least touch you? Nicely?"

"*Oh,* yes. Very, very nicely."

"Well then, if he's not smitten, I think he's at least been slapped around a little." Sherry smiled. She hoped Juliana's rush marriage would work out better than her own.

Not that Sherry's marriage was so bad. They got along fine. But if she could make herself stop wanting what she couldn't have, things would be a lot more comfortable.

"So you'll be there?" Juliana asked.

"Sure. We're both working nights. I'll twist Mike's arm and get him there. No problem."

Mike sighed when she told him about the wedding but made no other protest. It took place on the beach before the same judge who had married Mike and Sherry not quite two weeks earlier. He lifted an eyebrow when he recognized them and the bride, but made no comment otherwise.

Juliana's bridegroom had Sherry swallowing down envy. Not because Kurt Collier was possibly the prettiest man she'd ever seen. She far preferred Mike's hard-edged good looks to Kurt's gilded perfection. But Kurt behaved like a besotted bridegroom, gazing into Juliana's eyes, kissing her fingers as she spoke her vows, repeating his with a deep resonance that had Sherry fighting back tears. She was fairly certain Kurt's apparent devotion wasn't real, but he put on a good act. And who knew? Maybe she was wrong. Maybe he was sincere. Sherry hoped so. Juliana deserved some happiness. And so, damn it, did she.

But when the wedding was over, Mike had some kind of meeting. He gently detached his hand from Sherry's too-needy grasp and shook Kurt's in congratulations. He kissed Juliana's cheek and wished her well.

Sherry hugged everyone, accidentally on purpose including Mike in the hugs, and left with her husband, despite Juliana's invitation to join them for dinner. Kurt's obvious, unspoken gratitude when she turned them down made Sherry's envy swell up like an evil green toad, big enough to choke her.

She wanted that, wanted someone who was eager to be with her and only her. No, not just someone. She wanted it from Mike. Instead, he couldn't wait to get away from her.

Sherry dropped him off in front of the bank. He leaned back in before closing the door. "Don't bother coming to pick me up. I'll catch a ride or I'll walk. It's not far, and I'd rather you just went on to the club. People there can take care of any trouble."

She nodded and drove away before the car that was stopped behind her could honk. She wished she could feel special because Mike showed concern for her safety, but he did it for everyone.

Then she looked in the rear-view mirror and saw Tug

glaring at her from the driver's seat of the car following. Had he seen her? Was he following them? Maybe he didn't recognize her. She'd cut her hair, after all.

She drove a little farther down the street, fighting panic. He couldn't do anything to her now. Could he? Surely even Tug wasn't that crazy. In fact, they'd just passed the Palm Beach Police Department a few doors down from the bank. Realizing then what she should do, Sherry turned at the next block, past a row of businesses. Tug turned, too. She would circle back to the police station, and if Tug was still following her, she would park and go inside.

Just before she made the next turn, Tug pulled into a parking place along the street, and Sherry breathed a sigh of relief. Those phone calls had her a little too spooked.

On Friday night the party was just getting into full swing when Mike and Sherry arrived. People had spread through the house, drinking and laughing, getting geared up for a Palm Beach party. He could feel her hand tremble through his tuxedo sleeve. He laid his free hand over hers, where she'd tucked it into the crook of his elbow, and leaned down to murmur in her ear. "Spit in his eye. I'll back you up."

Her laugh sounded shaky, but he got one, as he'd hoped.

"I think I'll hold off on the saliva for now and just go for figurative spitting." She smiled up at him. "I think you'll do perfectly for that. He won't be able to abide knowing I'm married to you."

"My goal in life." He winked and led her up to the door.

It stood open to the balmy night air, his new relatives collected in the spacious entry hall beyond. Three of them—Sherry's sister, her new husband and the girls' father—Mike already knew. The tiny dark-haired woman with the dramatic coloring and the stretched look, hinting at more than one facelift, had to be the stepmother. He waited while Sherry kissed the air near the woman's cheek.

"Bebe. Tug." She didn't look at her father even as she called his name. "I'd like you to meet my husband, Micah Scott."

That was his cue. He stepped forward and offered his hand. "Pleased to meet you."

Bebe looked at his hand as if it were a dead fish washed up on the beach and took it in a two-fingered grasp, maybe worried that the fish smell would rub off. "How…nice to meet you, Mr. Scott. May I introduce—" She'd already let go to wave vaguely in her husband's direction.

"We've met." Mike extended his hand. Would the man take it? Mike almost wished he wouldn't. He was in the mood for a fight, verbal or otherwise, over the way they treated their daughter.

But Tug Nyland smiled a big fake toothy grin and clapped Mike on the shoulder as he pumped his hand, unable to resist the hard-squeeze-handshake competition under his jovial surface. "That's right. In front of that club, wasn't it? The day you two got married. Tell me, was it before we met, or after, that you married my daughter?"

Mike kept the smile pasted on his face. He knew it was small, tight and hard, but he couldn't fake it the way these people could. He nodded.

"Nyland," he said in both greeting and acknowledgment of the question. He didn't trust himself to say anything more.

"This is my other daughter." Nyland's tone of voice said "the good daughter." Mike clamped down harder on his mood.

"We already know each other." Juliana used Mike's outstretched hand to pull him in for a quick, fragrant hug. She looked different somehow. Softer. Prettier. Marriage must agree with her.

"I was at their wedding," Juliana was saying. "And they were at ours."

"You went to Sherry's wedding?" Nyland stifled his outrage, barely. "Why didn't you tell me? I'd have come. Helped celebrate."

Mike tucked Sherry against his side. He could feel her shaking, but none of it showed. He had no right to take pride in her gutsy attitude. She wasn't really his, except on paper. "Sherry wanted something small, very private," he said. "I agreed."

"What is it you do, Mr. Scott?" Bebe spoke, all polite refinement.

"Bodyguard?" Nyland put in his two cents.

"I work at La Jolie."

"A...bartender?" The stepmother actually staggered as she assumed the worst. In shock, Mike assumed, or maybe horror. She went pale. Nyland went a deeper shade of red.

"I do a lot of things there." Mike knew he only had to mention that he owned the club to soothe their sensibilities. Which was probably why he was enjoying this so much. "Sometimes I tend bar. Sometimes I do other things. Like deal with rowdy customers. Sherry's been working as hostess for us."

"Wor...worki—" Bebe stammered, her hand rising to her throat.

"Yes, working," Sherry said. "At La Jolie. It's fun." Beaming a big smile, she put her arm around Mike, beneath his jacket so that only his white silk shirt lay between her hand and his back.

The touch felt more intimate for being hidden. Mike wanted to move away but couldn't. This was the main purpose behind their imitation marriage. The show had to go on.

Bebe looked even more appalled. "Would...will any of—"

"I'm a friendly guy, Mrs. Nyland. I know a lot of people. On the other hand, the ones I have to…escort from the club are pretty drunk. They don't recognize faces too well under those conditions. Maybe they won't make the connection." Mike moved his hand up to Sherry's shoulder, thinking to get a little space between them.

He touched bare skin where the neckline of her shimmery dress swooped down Sherry's back to expose most of her shoulderblades. Somehow he managed to keep from jumping like one of those electrified frogs in the old experiments. She sent electricity slamming through him in just the same way.

Juliana laughed uncertainly. "Don't be so melodramatic, Bebe. Mike's family now. Just like Kurt." She pointed through the house. "The food is out back, near the pool. Find us later and we can talk."

With a last nod at their hosts, Mike led Sherry through the house, past the couples dancing in the sunroom-terrace with its row of glass-paned doors open to a courtyard where, as promised, they found food. He filled a plate with fresh boiled shrimp and steamed scallops, choosing the things he could recognize from the buffet table. Over the years, he'd become a connoisseur of the exotic when it came to food, but he preferred knowing what he was eating, or at least knowing the chef.

"Why, Sherry Nyland, as I live and breathe. Do introduce your friend." The sugary-sweet, fake-magnolia voice belonged to a short voluptuous blonde. The other reason, the main reason, he hated these parties—the people who came to them.

"It's Sherry Scott," Mike said, not bothering to extend his hand. "I'm her husband."

"Her…" The blonde looked from Sherry to Mike and back again. "My goodness, you Nyland girls are just full of surprises tonight, aren't you? Wherever did you find him?''

Sherry threaded her arm through Mike's. ''Doesn't matter. There aren't any more like him. He's one of a kind.''

''That's too bad.'' The woman dipped her forefinger in her drink and ran it down her cleavage, giving him a ''come hither'' look from her heavy-lidded eyes. ''I guess we'll just have to make do with the one.''

''Sorry.'' Mike turned away. ''Not interested.''

He found a quiet corner where he could eat his seafood in peace. Sherry came with him.

''Go visit with your friends,'' he told her. ''I'm sure you want to. As long as you stay outside, I can keep an eye on you from here.'' He needed a little space. All the touching and holding they'd done had him wanting more than was safe.

Sherry popped a tiny tomato in her mouth. ''These are all Tug and Bebe's friends. Not mine. I never did much of the Palm Beach social whirl. Most of my friends live in places like New York or Atlanta for most of the year.''

''Why do you live here, then?''

She gave him a one-shoulder shrug. ''I'm not sure anymore. Every time I talked about moving away, hunting for a job, going back to school, Tug went on and on about how hard it was, how dangerous the city was, things like that. It seemed— I thought it meant he wanted me, wanted me nearby, anyway. So I stayed.''

Mike wondered what it was that Tug had really wanted. The man obviously didn't care about his daughter beyond the money he could get out of her. Mike could tell Sherry had been hurt when she finally realized that truth, but he didn't think she would welcome his sympathy.

''Anyway—'' she turned a new bright smile on him ''—I thought the whole idea behind coming to this party was to demonstrate how madly in love we are. How can we do that if I'm over there and you're over here?''

Damn. She was right. ''You have a point.'' He managed a brief cockeyed smile. ''Guess you're stuck, then.''

''Oh, I wouldn't call it stuck.'' Sherry took his empty plate and set it on a nearby tray. ''Dance with me?''

She drew him by both hands to the dance floor set up beyond the pool. The band was playing something slow and romantic he remembered from high school. He didn't want to do this. Didn't need to do it.

And just like every other time in the past few weeks, Mike found himself doing exactly what he knew he shouldn't. He took Sherry into his arms, laid his cheek against hers and moved to the music.

The world floated away. Or maybe they were the ones floating, rising above the palms and party lights to dance among the stars. Step by tiny step, Sherry moved closer. Mike spread his hand wide on the small of her back, touching as much of her as he could reach. His other hand held hers, tucked against his chest.

Her short hair drifted against his face in the offshore breeze, an inadvertent caress, and he had to take a deep breath. The scent that was uniquely Sherry mixed with that of the sea and summer jasmine, making him light-headed. Or was that caused by her body moving against his? He didn't know, nor did he care. He could go on dancing like this till the world came to an end.

Sherry sighed. Her hand on his shoulder slid upward until it curved around his neck above his collar, and her fingers slid into his hair. She stroked her cheek against his, her soft against his rough. He didn't know it was possible to want anyone so much.

Someone tapped him on the shoulder. ''Can I cut in?'' A woman's voice. Mike stared down at her a full minute before he recognized Juliana.

She laughed. "Did you even hear the music? You danced through three songs exactly the same. Even the Metallica one."

He could feel his face burn and hoped the lights were dim enough it didn't show. At least people would believe they were typical newlyweds. "Do you want to dance?"

"Actually I want to steal my sister for a few minutes." Juliana linked her arm through Sherry's. "But I'm sure you won't have any problem finding a partner."

"Thanks. Think I'll pass." Mike followed them back toward the house.

The sisters settled into a wicker sofa in the glassed-in sunroom to talk. Mike spotted a bar set up at the other end of the narrow room and moved that way. He could keep an inconspicuous eye on Sherry from there.

He waved away the offered champagne. It had never been his drink of choice. But Sherry looked to be settled in for a long cozy chat, and he didn't want to just stand here holding up the wall, so he asked for a beer—and was a little surprised to get one. He took the bottle, waving off the glass, deciding to go in-your-face with his lower-class origins. He might be as rich or richer, than these people, but he wasn't one of them.

Mike moved to one of the shoulder-wide sections of wall between the wide-open glass doors, hoping to get away from the bar traffic. He leaned back against the wall, lifted one foot and propped it against the wall, too. The party flowed in and out of the house in waves between his position and Sherry's. Glittering people, groomed within an inch of their lives, talking maniacally about nothing at all. Mike fitted in about as well as a wolf in a pack of poodles.

He took a sip of his beer and watched his wife as she talked with her sister. Did Sherry have a clue how gorgeous she was? Her skirt rode high on her thighs as she sat with her feet curled under her, her shoes lying on the floor. Mike wanted to tug her skirt down, cover up those legs all the way to her ankles and hide them from every guy in the place. Including himself.

He tipped the bottle to his lips again and saw his father-in-law steaming across the gray stone floor toward him.

Nine

Mike dropped his foot to the floor, but didn't change his casual lean against the wall.

"So you and my Sherry are really married." Tug rattled the ice in his drink—whiskey from the smell of it.

"Yep. Legally binding and all that."

Mike waited, watching Sherry, while Tug stared at him. He didn't know what the man wanted, but as long as he stayed away from Sherry, Mike didn't particularly care.

"Why?" Tug said. "What do you think you'll get out of it?"

Stupid question. Mike looked at the other man. "A wife."

Tug went on as if Mike hadn't spoken. "You're planning on raking in a tidy pile on her birthday, I'm sure. Maybe you'd better make other plans. Divorce her now, and I'll make it worth your while. Otherwise you'll get nothing."

Temper flaring, Mike somehow managed to keep from

grabbing his father-in-law by the throat. "Sherry is my wife. You got that? *Mine.* And not you or any of these other spoiled, greedy SOBs is going to change that."

The older man's face went red. "Who the hell do you think you are? You're nothing, that's what. Nothing and nobody."

"Maybe so," Mike said. "But I'm the nobody who is Sherry's husband. And I'm not going away."

Tug flushed a deeper crimson, and before Mike could react, the burly man swung. His fist blasted into Mike's face, snapping his head aside. The second blow came right behind it from the other direction. Mike stopped the third, catching his father-in-law's wrist and twisting it behind his back in a familiar, well-practiced move.

Women were screaming, guests both scrambling away and gathering to watch. Sherry's voice carried above the crowd and Mike looked up to see her shoving her way through the crowd toward him. She called his name.

Mike twisted Tug's arm higher, applying the pressure he'd long ago learned would immobilize the most powerful foe. He leaned forward and whispered in the man's ear. "Stay away from Sherry and stay away from me, and we'll get along just fine. Understand?"

Tug sputtered, tried more threats, saying, "Do you know who I am?" unwilling to give up just yet.

Mike increased the pressure. "Stay away from Sherry, or you'll be dealing with me. Do you understand?"

"Yes, yes, all right."

The minute Tug's bluster collapsed, Mike released him, watched him retreat until he felt Sherry reach his side.

"Oh, Micah—" She touched his cheek, near the ache he could feel swelling. "What happened?"

He looked around at the still-growing crowd and shrugged. "Caused a scene, looks like."

"Who cares about that? Your face—does it hurt much?"

She brushed fingers lightly across the ache, and Mike had to suppress a shudder.

Not from pain. Her touch didn't hurt, exactly. He felt it, was aware of it, but the shudder came from her careful gentleness. It affected him in ways he didn't want it to.

"Let's get out of here." He took Sherry's elbow to urge her out the front door.

"Yes. We need to get that eye looked at."

"No, forget it. Let's just go home."

Sherry pulled her arm from his grasp. "Absolutely not. Not until I know how your eye is."

"It's fine."

"I don't believe you. Let me see it." She caught his face and tried to turn it toward her.

Mike jerked his head back and stepped away. "Not here. People are staring."

"Let them stare."

"Let's go."

"Fine. The kitchen's that way."

"I want out of this house." He couldn't stay here among these parasites another second.

Sherry took him by the wrist and led him out the open doors to the backyard.

"The car's that way." Mike pointed back through the house. He needed to get away from all the staring and gossip.

"I refuse to wait till we get home to see what Tug's done to you, and the light's bad in the car. There's a pool house."

He saw it then, the rough-hewn wood siding hidden behind overgrown bushes. Sherry dragged him around the pool and up the walkway into the small building. Mike kicked the door shut behind him. He didn't want anyone to know the pool house was occupied. She kept going across the room, not bothering to turn on lights.

Finally Sherry went through another door, flipped a light switch and Mike found himself in a spartan, gray-tiled bathroom.

"Sit there." She pointed at the toilet as she rummaged in a cabinet.

Mike put the seat down and did as she ordered. Before Mike knew what she intended, she was bending over him, turning his face up to the light.

She wet a cloth in the sink and dabbed it over his bruises. The cool water felt good. "What happened?"

"Stupidity." He tried to use his disgust at his own actions to wall off the feelings rising inside him. It didn't work.

Sherry stood far too close to him in her shiny stockings and her shimmery party dress; her head bent over his, trying to clean up the results of his own foolishness. And he couldn't stop himself from wanting to haul her onto his lap and kiss her. Her tender concern made his own tenderness well up, strong and uncrushable. It was why this whole mess had happened in the first place. He couldn't stop the feelings, no matter how hard he tried. They kept coming back.

When Sherry's father had said those rude things at the party, absolute fury had swept through Mike so fast, it was all he could do to control it. He never would have been so angry, had he not felt more for Sherry than he should. He'd spouted off, which made things worse. He hadn't thrown any punches, but if he'd kept his cool, most likely nothing would have happened.

He couldn't deny it anymore. He had feelings for her. Feelings that grew stronger with every little hiss that escaped her as she tried to bathe his wounds without hurting him. The bruises didn't hurt nearly as much as *he* would when all this was over, especially if he didn't get control of himself now. He wasn't in love with her, not yet. But

all the pieces were there—the tenderness, the protective-
ness, the desire.

Mike leaned forward just enough to breathe in her scent.
He had to get away, had to get her safely home, had to get
some distance from her unknowing temptation, or he would
break something else—his promise to himself. His heart.

Sherry tossed the cloth in the sink. "You're lucky," she
said. "I don't see any skin broken. Not even a busted lip."

"He missed my mouth." A bit of fortune for which Mike
was becoming more grateful by the minute.

"What happened? Why did he hit you?"

"I wouldn't divorce you."

"Oh." She looked away, fidgeting with a fold of her
dress. "I'm so sorry."

"Why? It's not your fault your father's pond scum."

She gave a little forlorn one-shoulder shrug. "It's my
fault you have to deal with him."

"I don't mind." Mike could resist no longer. He needed
her in his arms, needed it like he needed air. He tugged her
off balance, into his lap. "I don't mind at all," he said as
he touched his mouth to hers.

The kiss was pure sweetness and heartache, and Mike
couldn't make himself change its tone. He felt what he felt,
and it all came out in the kiss—sweet, hot and pure.

Her hand settled on his cheek, a drift of warm comfort.
She sighed, relaxing into his embrace, sending Mike high
and tight with this evidence of her trust. He wanted—
needed more. Anything she would give him.

So what if it broke every policy he'd ever laid out for
himself? He didn't care anymore how stupid it was to get
any deeper involved with her. He didn't care that she'd
grown up in Palm Beach. At this moment all he cared about
was that Sherry was his wife and she was in his arms.

Mike slid his hand down her waist, past the curve of her
hip, until he reached the hem of her dress. There he waited,

his hand on her nylons-covered thigh, for a sign from Sherry. Would she object?

Her breathy moan didn't sound like an objection. Nor did her gasp when he brushed his thumb under the edge of her skirt. She deepened the kiss, stroking her tongue into his mouth. Her hand slid from his cheek down inside his jacket, where she pressed it to his chest.

He leaned back, and the plumbing fixtures digging into his spine reminded him where they were. In a bathroom. He lurched to his feet, setting Sherry down on hers as he did, because he wasn't sure he wouldn't drop her. He didn't let go, though, as he staggered toward the doorway.

She wrapped her arms around his neck and clung like a limpet. She kissed his throat, his chin, his cheek, and Mike had to stop his unsteady progress to kiss her mouth again, drawing her up tight against his body. One hand found her bottom, cupped its firm curves, used it to hold her where he needed her. But he never forgot his goal. He wanted out of the bathroom.

Sherry panicked when Mike started moving once more. It didn't matter that he kept his arms around her, walked her with him. He'd done that before and still walked away. She couldn't take it happening again.

"Mike. Wait." She punctuated her words with kisses.

He groaned and propped his forehead on hers. "What?" He brushed her hair aside with his nose and nibbled at her earlobe, almost driving all thought from her mind.

"What's wrong?" she gasped.

"Nothing." His nibbling moved down her neck, and Sherry dropped her head back to give him better access. His lips plucked lightly at her skin, leaving behind a moist trail that made her shiver.

"Then, where—" She forgot the rest of what she wanted to say when he pushed a knee between hers and suckled lightly at a spot just beneath her jaw. Her skirt was too straight to let him put the pressure of his knee where she wanted it, unless she hiked it up. Did she dare?

"We're in the bathroom." He rushed the words out and returned to his nibbling.

"So?" She couldn't manage more.

Mike slipped his hand from her bottom to her thigh and began inching her skirt up for her. "So I refuse to make love to my wife for the first time in a bathroom."

Oh, dear heaven. Jolted by his words, Sherry shoved his jacket halfway down his back, reveling in the feel of his powerful shoulders beneath smooth silk. She buzzed with the need to touch. He was so broad, so strong, so much more than anything she'd ever known.

"That is…" He paused. "If *you* want—"

"There's a bed." She didn't care if it made her sound needy. She was needy. Well beyond the point where pride could have any effect.

"Thank God." Mike lifted her in his arms. Not sweeping her off her feet like Rhett carrying Scarlett up the stairs, but straight up in the air, body to body, heat to heat. Sherry wrapped her legs around him, hiking her skirt up the rest of the way. Mike kissed her, his tongue plunging deep, making promises she hoped he would finally keep.

"Where?" he gasped.

"Turn right." Her voice didn't sound any clearer than his. "You can't miss it."

He went through the doorway and turned right. Two quick strides later he bumped the bed and fell on to it with her. They kissed, necks straining, lips reaching, unable to break apart, as they scrambled to rid themselves of clothing, hands jumping from one to the other.

He tugged his tie loose, while she unbuttoned his shirt, stopping after only three buttons when he broke the kiss long enough to whip the tie over his head. He lowered the zipper on the back of her dress, while she yanked his tuxedo jacket inside out, trying to pull it off his arms, unable to see because her mouth was so deeply involved with his.

Her dress came off in one violent struggle, and they came together again, clinging as if they'd been parted for years rather than seconds. She wriggled her panty hose halfway down, then finished undoing his shirt buttons, his belt buckle and his slacks as he peeled her stockings the rest of the way off.

Then, finally, Sherry glued her naked body to Mike's. The touch of his skin against hers made her quiver with anticipation. His erection trapped between them told her she wouldn't have long to wait. But it told her wrong.

All of Mike's desperate haste vanished. His kiss somehow softened and deepened at the same time, becoming both passionate and tender. He cupped her face in both his hands as he kissed her. Then he lifted his head and looked at her, gazing into her eyes a long moment before turning to watch as his hand skimmed down her neck, out her shoulder and back to cover her breast. He followed the path of his touch with his eyes.

Sherry felt no urge to cover herself, though she felt exposed and vulnerable under Mike's gaze. He made her feel sexy, wanton, beautiful, safe. He had promised. She was safe with him.

Micah lowered his head, touched his lips to her neck, and Sherry quivered. He kissed his way down to her shoulder, his fingers skimming over her skin just ahead of his kisses. She squirmed, her breasts tingling. She needed him to touch her there, but he wouldn't. Slowly, inch by inch, he moved across her shoulders, nipping at her collarbone, dropping a damp, tender kiss in the hollow of her throat and another in the dip above the slender bone on the other side.

Only then did he move lower, kissing his way across the upper slopes of her breasts and into the valley between.

Sherry arched her back, begging silently for more. Her nipples had tightened into hard little buds in anticipation of Mike's slow sensual journey, and still he passed them by, lavishing his kisses everywhere else. He followed the path set by his hands, around her breasts, across her stomach, along the sensitive inner surface of her upper arms. Every touch, every kiss tantalized her, brought her nerves to quivering life and left her hungry for more.

When his palm brushed over the peak of her breast, she jerked convulsively, galvanized by the electricity of his touch. Or perhaps it was her own need for his touch that made her jump. She'd never felt this much. She didn't know what to do with all the feelings he created inside her. There wasn't room in her body to hold it all in. There wasn't room in her heart for everything Micah Scott made her feel.

His mouth closed hot and wet over her breast and she cried out, muffling the sound with her hand. The tip of his tongue teased the tip of her breast, flicking back and forth. It sent sparks shooting to the hollow inside her that wept to be filled. She spread her legs, pushed her knee between his, trying without words to tell him what she wanted. Micah's only response was to turn the same careful attention to her other breast.

She would go crazy. She wasn't made to endure so much sheer delight. Sherry thrust her fingers into his hair, not sure whether she meant to push him away or hold him in place. It didn't seem to matter. Mike kissed wherever he wanted.

He turned her onto her stomach to press kisses to the tender backs of her knees. It tickled in a way that sent more sparks to arouse her further.

"It's too much," she whispered, unable to bear any more.

"There's no such thing." His fingers traced lines of fire up her thighs. "It's not enough."

His lips followed where his fingers led, sometimes kissing, sometimes just sliding enticingly along her skin. Now and again his tongue would lick out as if to taste a particularly tempting spot on her body. Sherry trembled in anticipation, waiting for his next little erotic taste.

He kissed her thighs and her calves, her back and the arches of her feet. He kissed her bottom, his breath sliding warm down her curves to make her tremble even more. It was as if he intended to memorize every part of her. Why? It made no sense, unless he intended this to be their only time together.

She couldn't bear it. She needed him now. Sherry rolled to her back. "Make love to me, Micah." She tried to pull him up over her, but he refused to budge.

"I am." His fingers combed through the fine blond hair between her legs to find her warm wet secrets. "I will. I promise."

Surely he wouldn't continue his pattern now, his hand leading where his mouth would follow. But he did. Sherry came up off the bed at the electrifying slide of his tongue across her sensitized bud. What was he doing to her?

The world slid away, her body tensed, poised on the edge of some unimaginable cliff. The second touch sent her flying, exploding into a million scattering sparks. But it wasn't enough. She needed more, needed him inside her, and he gave her what she needed in one deep thrust.

He rose over her, elbows straight. She set her hands on his chest simply to touch him in return. Her eyes drifted shut as he began a driving rhythm, pushing her toward that spectacular short circuit once more.

She tossed her head, trying to hold back. She couldn't take it, not again. She knew this time would be magnified far beyond the first, just seconds ago.

He caught her hips and lifted them higher. "Feel it, Sherry. Let go. Fly with me."

"I can't." She was almost sobbing as the sensations built. It was too much.

"You can. Trust me." He sounded much like she did, his voice broken with effort and...and something else. Something more. "I'll be here. Catch you when you come down. Promise."

"Micah, please—" She begged for mercy, but he had none.

"Let go."

"I can't," she cried at the moment the explosion overtook her. Time stood still, shattered around her, as her body convulsed with pleasure.

His cry echoed hers. Did he say her name? She didn't know, couldn't tell. He'd overwhelmed all her senses so nothing got through but what he made her feel. She still trembled in its aftermath when Mike curled down over her, holding his weight up on shaky elbows for a few moments before rolling to the side, taking her with him.

She wanted to put her arms around him, but hadn't the strength. What had he done to her?

He stroked his cheek along hers, then kissed her just in front of her ear, and her tears came back.

Now still, even after it was over, he was so sweet. Because making love was more than just "the act," exactly as he'd told her. It began long before and, apparently, lingered afterward. And Mike's devotion to her pleasure showed her something. Sherry knew he didn't love her, but he cared. More than anyone had ever cared about her before.

He had fed her a seven-course meal of caring, and all she was used to getting was the odd cup of gruel now and again. No wonder it had seemed too much. He had filled her to overflowing. And now her tears overflowed, despite her efforts to hold back.

"Sherry? What's wrong?" Mike sounded on the verge of panic.

She couldn't speak, could only twine her arms around his neck, hide her face against his shoulder and cry.

"Are you all right? Did I hurt you?" He alternated between trying to see her face and holding her close.

Sherry nodded her head, then shook it. Yes to the first question. No to the second. Maybe she should have just said no. No, she wasn't all right. Then again, maybe she had never been all right before; but now, for once, she was.

"Talk to me, Sherry." He smoothed her hair back from her forehead and twisted around until he could kiss her there. "Tell me what's wrong."

"Nothing," she whispered. "Everything is right."

She could feel him shake his head. Undoubtedly he didn't understand. Sherry didn't exactly understand herself. But he tucked her head against his shoulder and cradled her there while she cried. He stroked her hair, pressing the occasional kiss to the top of her head or to her arm wrapped around his neck, and he waited.

At last, her tears began to subside. Sherry lay boneless in Mike's arms, her legs twined with his, and listened to the music seeping in through the closed windows.

"Feel better?" His fingers combing through her hair felt heavenly.

"Mmm." She wiped her eyes on his bare chest and looked up at him. "I hate to cry."

"What brought all that on?" He stroked his thumb beneath each of her eyes in turn, removing the last trace of dampness. "Me?"

"Sort of."

The dismay in his face made her heart turn over again. "No." She took his face between her hands and kissed him, just a little tender kiss. She kissed his eyes and his cheeks. "You were wonderful. Better than perfect. That's why."

He still didn't look as if he believed her. She would have to explain. She couldn't bear for him to be hurt, even a tiny bit.

"Do you know where my name came from? Sherry?" She smoothed down his rumpled up eyebrows. "Not exactly the usual run-of-the-mill name here in Palm Beach is it?"

He shrugged.

Sherry took a deep breath. She had to get it all out at once or she never would. "Actually I'm lucky that sherry was considered an acceptable drink for young ladies when my mom was growing up. At least it *sounds* like a normal, ordinary name. I might have wound up named 'Whiskey' or 'Vodka', or maybe 'Tequila.' But my mom didn't discover those till I was older. She cared more about her 'drinkies' than she did about me. She fell off a boat at anchor in the harbor and drowned because she was drunk. Then I came to live with Tug and Bebe. I guess you have a pretty good idea what that was like."

He didn't say anything, just stroked his thumb under her eyes.

"Don't you understand?" she whispered. "You cared. You saw me. Just me. Nobody else ever did that."

Mike drew her in. He was in deep, deep water here, with the wind rising. He kissed her forehead before he tucked her close again and held her. He'd known all along that if he ever made love to her it would change everything. Her whispered confession only intensified the change. How could he let her go?

And yet he knew he had to do it in the end. She might have recognized that he cared about her, but she had said nothing about caring for him in return. Tonight had crumbled his defensive walls, and somehow he had to build them up again so that when the time came, he could say goodbye with a little dignity.

But what if he didn't have to? What if she decided to stay? If she fell in love with him—

No. He couldn't delude himself. Blair had loved him. She'd said so, anyway. But she'd loved his money more. And when she found a guy with even more money than he had, she was gone.

Sherry was different. He knew that. But he didn't dare take the chance that she was different enough. Much as it had hurt when he discovered the truth about Blair, he knew already that Sherry could hurt him even more. He had to be prepared, had to be ready to open his arms and let her walk away.

"They'll be wondering where we are." Sherry spoke against his chest. It tickled a little.

He rubbed the spot. "Probably so."

"We should get dressed. Go back to the party."

He didn't want to. If he stayed here, holding her naked in his arms, the end might not come. "You're right."

Reluctantly, slowly, hands lingering as they drew apart, Mike got out of bed. He explored the open room in the light spilling through the bathroom doorway, hunting their wide-flung clothes. He put his on, tossed Sherry's in her direction. He found the discarded protection and disposed of it in the bathroom trash.

"My dress is all crumpled." Sherry stood scowling at herself in the bathroom mirror. "And my hair—"

Mike grinned, coming to stand behind her, looking at their reflection together. "That's the good thing about your new hairstyle, isn't it? It always looks like you just got out of bed, so when you really did just get out of bed…"

She turned around and pinched his arm through the tux. "Hush."

His grin faded and he fought the urge to kiss her again as she gazed up at him.

"This was the most beautiful experience I've ever known," she said, not quite whispering.

"Yeah." He nodded. "Me, too." He swallowed down the emotion trying to break free. "But you know—" he had to stop and clear his throat "—you know it can't happen again."

She touched his mouth, her fingers tracing lightly across his lips. He kissed them. He had to.

"I know," she said. "Too bad."

The urge took over his body, hands moving to hold her, head lowering. He kissed her once more, deep and hot, with all the passion he still felt. At the door to the pool house, at his last opportunity, he kissed her one last time. He cupped the soft curve of her cheek in his hand, laced the fingers of the other through hers and kissed her with everything that was in his heart, slow and sweet and tender.

Then he opened the door and they went back out into the world.

The next few weeks passed in a painful blur. Mike moved Sherry back to the day shift, claiming that with Clara back home she needed watching at night. In reality, he did it to make it easier for him to avoid Sherry.

It helped that they had two cars now and didn't have to chauffeur each other around. Sherry had simply walked into her father's office at the party, claimed the keys to her car and driven it home.

In one sense, all the changes worked. He seldom saw her. But that didn't seem to matter. Sherry was always there, whether she was physically present or not. She was a constant ache in his heart.

So he would get over it. He had no other choice. He had

to endure it, get through it, and eventually the pain would go away. He hoped.

Late on a Wednesday night, Mike was working in his office as usual when the phone rang.

"Micah?" Sherry sounded tentative, almost afraid of him. He'd never intended that.

"I'm here." He tried to gentle his tone, but didn't know how well he succeeded when just hearing her voice made his body tighten.

"You need to come down to the hospital. Clara's fine, but—"

He didn't hear anything more. He'd already flung the phone in the direction of its cradle and headed down the stairs.

Ten

Sherry met him at the emergency room door. "She's fine, Micah, truly. Feisty as ever."

She pulled his hand from its too-tight grasp on her elbow and held it as she led him through the maze of treatment rooms. "That's why I called you. She's arguing with the doctor and the nurses and anyone else who will hold still long enough."

"Then why is she here?" He wanted to shake her, put his fist through the wall, do something to get rid of the lingering panic, but he clamped down on the urge.

"She fainted. I caught her, so she didn't break anything, but—well, I guess I panicked." Sherry made a face. "That's why I came out here to wait for you, because Clara was yelling at me for calling 911. I think it embarrassed her to be wheeled out of the building on a stretcher."

"Thank you. You did the right thing. She can stand a little embarrassment." Mike looked up at her then, truly focused on her for the first time since he'd arrived at the hospital.

A bruise darkened her left cheekbone and a black eye was beginning to develop above it.

He frowned. "What happened to you?"

"Nothing." She waved his question away.

Mike stopped and pulled her around to face him, touching the puffy bruises with gentle fingers. "It doesn't look like nothing to me. What happened?"

"Your mother is waiting." Sherry pointed at the door just behind her through which the reassuring sound of familiar voices came.

"I know. I can hear her. You said she was fine. Isn't she?"

"Well, yes. Basically. The doctor said—"

"I'll ask him myself in a minute. Now, tell me what happened to your face." He brushed back her hair and tipped her chin up, turning the discoloration to the light.

Sherry pulled away, refusing to meet his searching gaze. "Your mother's heavier than she looks. When she fainted—" she shrugged "—I lost my balance. We both went down, and the kitchen island got in my way. But Clara's fine."

Mike's throat went so tight it hurt to breathe. He gathered Sherry into his arms, ignoring her stiff resistance, and held her close until his heart decided it didn't need to pound its way out of his chest after all. This woman had not only taken care of his mother, she'd sacrificed herself doing it. And she was his wife.

How was he going to let her go? He could always get her to stay by telling the truth about his finances, but he didn't want her on those terms. He needed to push her away, prove to her that they came from two different worlds that could never overlap. And maybe, if the pushing didn't work—

No. They were too different. He would prove it to himself, as well, if he had to.

He pushed away from her and went through the door into the treatment room.

His mother glared at him past a tangle of wires and tubes. "It's about time you got here. Take me home, this instant."

"Hell, no, I'm not taking you home," he retorted, knowing she wouldn't respond to soothing words. "You blacked my wife's eye when you fainted. You deserve a week's torture in the hospital as payback."

"I wouldn't exactly call it torture," the doctor protested.

"Neither would I. But my mother does." Mike introduced himself to the emergency room physician. "What happened?"

Sherry stood on the fringes of the room and watched her husband in action. Clara's blood pressure medicine would have to be adjusted, and the doctor thought her regular cardiologist, who was on his way in, would probably recommend a pacemaker, but she really was all right. Or as all right as she could be, given the circumstances. Sherry clung to that knowledge. She hadn't totally screwed up.

Of course Clara didn't want the pacemaker, didn't want to be electrocuted a hundred times a day, didn't want any fuss. She most especially did not want to stay in the hospital for any length of time, much less overnight. Mike overrode her objections to the hospital, told her they'd discuss the pacemaker later and soothed his sisters when they came flying in. His skill left Sherry marveling.

A passing nurse handed her an ice pack for her eye, but the shiver that swept through her had nothing to do with the cold. She could still feel Mike's touch, feel the warmth of his arms around her, the throb of his heart beating against hers. She wanted more, and the depth of that wanting scared her.

It was happening all over again. The same old pattern.

She was willing to turn herself inside out for a few drops of attention. It had to stop. And yet, and yet...

Mike was different. He had made love to *her*. To Sherry Eloise Nyland Scott, not to some available body. She could swear it had happened that way, that she hadn't just imagined his passionate care. For her and no one else. How could she think of never having that again, ever, for the rest of her life?

But how could she let herself experience it again, knowing it couldn't last? Wouldn't it make her all the more needy? All the more willing to follow him around like some old dog begging to have its ears scratched?

Then again, she was stronger now. She'd broken away from her father. He hadn't made a single phone call to either Mike's house or Clara's since the party, but if he did, she'd tell him just what she thought. Granted, the break had required drastic acts on both their parts—his despicable plan plus her desperate reaction—to make it happen, but she knew better now. She knew she could make it alone. She knew she could do whatever she had to. So what harm could she come to by making love to Mike again? What could it hurt?

A few more weeks passed before Mike could put his plan into action. His mother's blood pressure was back where it needed to be, but she was still resisting the pacemaker. She wouldn't move in with him, wouldn't let any of the family come stay with her, so he hired a private-duty nurse. She complained about that, too, but he ignored the complaints. If she needed a keeper, he'd make sure she had one.

Finally, bright but not so early, on a Saturday morning, Mike pulled up in front of a big, two-story frame house and got out of his car. Sherry exited from the other side and came around to stare up at the Key West–style house with its porches spanning the front of the house on both floors. "We're painting *that?*"

He laughed. His plan would work wonderfully. "Just the inside. The exterior paint ought to be good for another year or two, providing we don't get another hurricane. We do have to paint the porch floors. They wear through pretty quick." The messy job ought to show her quickly that she didn't fit into his life.

"And why are we painting it again? I mean you and me doing the job, not why does it need painting." She hitched up her borrowed, too-big painting shorts.

"Because it's cheaper if we do it. Costs too much money to have somebody else do what we can do ourselves." This was perfect. She even gave him the opening to emphasize their many differences. He might have money enough to hire painters these days, but he'd done it himself plenty of times. Surely his cheapskate attitude would help drive her away.

"No, I understand that. I mean—why this house? What does this house have to do with us? With you?"

"Didn't I say?" Mike opened the trunk of his car to get out the approximately one-zillion gallons of paint. "Mom owns it. I grew up in this house."

"You did?" Sherry had to use both hands, but she helped lift the cans out of the trunk.

"Yep. When I moved back to West Palm Beach, I moved in here with them. But after Dad died, Mom said I needed my own place and she did, too. Her health wasn't as good by then, and I thought she'd be better off someplace smaller where I could still keep an eye on her.

"So we moved into the apartments and she started renting this house out. The renters just moved, and the place has to be cleaned up for the next batch. Paint is just the beginning." He gave her a wicked grin, thinking of all the carpet cleaning, vinyl polishing and bathroom scrubbing yet to come.

She rolled her eyes at him and started lugging cans of paint to the porch.

He decided to start upstairs in the bedrooms. Standard white paint made the house easier to rent, though harder to keep clean. Sherry spread the drop cloths, he put up the ladder. The twelve-foot ceilings required it, even with a long handle on the roller.

Sherry was assigned the woodwork, and after some basic instruction, turned out to be pretty good at it. He could cover more territory faster with the roller, so he ended up finishing the wide baseboards alongside her. Her hands and forearms were covered with tiny paint speckles, she had a big splotch of paint in her hair—his fault—and a smear along her cheek she'd done herself. She was a mess. His plan was working perfectly and it put him in a good mood.

They moved to the next bedroom. Mike loaded the roller with paint.

"Let me try." Sherry grabbed the handle, but was smart enough not to yank it. "I want to do this part."

"Why?"

"Because." She tugged, and he let go, reluctantly.

"Careful. Don't get too much paint on it."

"I know that." She picked at the paint in her hair. "Mr. Drip-the-Paint-on-His-Wife."

"It'll come out."

"It better." Sherry narrowed her eyes at him, but he thought she might be teasing. He hoped she wasn't. He wanted her unhappy, and she seemed entirely too cheerful.

She rolled the paint on, leaving speckled gaps behind.

"Press harder," he said.

"Like this?" She tried again, with marginally better results.

"Harder." Mike reached around her to grab the metal

pole and apply the proper pressure. "When you use a roller, you more or less mash the paint on the wall."

A smooth stripe of paint, appeared and Sherry laughed. "Oh, that is so cool. The wall's all dingy and dirty, and presto! It's all pretty and white."

She still held the paint roller, admiring the single stripe of paint while the paint dried on the roller, and while he, Mike suddenly realized, still held Sherry. His hands were on the roller, but his arms were around her.

He let go of the handle, but couldn't back away. Not with her scent filling up his head like helium and her nape right there in front of him needing to be kissed.

What had happened to his plan? He'd been so sure it would work, he'd let down his guard and she'd crawled in over it.

"I want to paint colors. Blue. I want blue. And red. I want to paint something red." She whirled around, almost whacking him in the head with the paint roller. "I never got colors before. Bebe redecorated every other year, but always white walls, what she wanted. Never what I wanted. My opinion never mattered. Ever."

"Easy." He took the roller away from her and leaned it against the wall, trying not to think about the little girl who hadn't mattered. "And let's stick with white here, okay? You can paint the apartment whatever color you want."

"You mean it?" The excitement shining in her eyes made his heart pound faster.

He shrugged. "Sure. Why not? It's only paint. If we go blind from all the color, we just paint it again."

"Oh, Mike." Now there were tears in her eyes. How was he supposed to fight tears?

Sherry threw her arms around his neck and kissed him so fiercely he staggered back a pace before he caught her up against him and returned the kiss with equal fervor. His need exploded, as if the past endless weeks of control had only added fuel to his smoldering fire, ready to catch the instant she stirred him up.

He pushed both hands inside her baggy shorts, to cup her bottom over the filmy panties she wore, and hauled her up hard against him. Not enough. He laid her down on the worn, paint-spattered old sheet that served as a drop cloth and cupped her breast in his hand. Not enough. He shoved her T-shirt and bra up out of his way and claimed her breast, pulling her nipple deep into his mouth, and still it wasn't enough. Would never be enough, because he wanted her. Sherry. Not just her breathtaking body.

Mike tugged the T-shirt back down over her breast and lay there with his head where it was, gasping for breath, praying for strength. "Can't," he croaked.

Sherry's fingers combed through his hair. "Why?"

He could hear the tears in her voice. *Please don't cry.* He couldn't handle that. He'd break in a million pieces if she cried.

"Why, Mike?" she whispered.

"Because." Stupid answer. He had to do better. He owed her that much. It might be easier if he could let go of her. Then again, maybe not. "I told you. It has to mean something. To both of us."

"But I know you care—" She broke off, her hand stilled on his head.

He couldn't take this. He broke away from her, stood up and walked away, but not far. Just to the door leading out to the second-story porch where he looked out at the street. He heard Sherry moving around behind him. Maybe she'd leave now, leave him to his misery. No such luck.

She touched his shoulder. "Mike?"

He tried to shrug her off, but she wouldn't go. She took his arm, and he let her tug him around to face her. He couldn't look at her, though, staring past her at the other door. Her fingers tracing feather soft down his cheek made his eyes close against the sweetness.

"Can you possibly think I don't—" Her voice wasn't any louder than a whisper, but he heard her. "You do, though, don't you? Oh, Micah."

Her hands rested on his chest as she stretched up and kissed his mouth. He didn't kiss her back—somehow—but his hands came up to cover hers.

She kissed his cheek right next to his mouth. "You have no idea how much I care."

She stepped away from him then, and he let her go, the way he would have to when the time came. She grasped the hem of her T-shirt and took it off, then reached behind her to unhook her bra. With a little shimmy, she dropped it to the floor.

What was she doing? Mike stood frozen, staring, as she skimmed her shorts and panties down to the floor and stepped out of them. Why?

He couldn't move, couldn't think, couldn't talk as she walked back to him. What did she want? Whatever it was, it was hers. Anything she wanted. She was so beautiful.

Sherry took the hem of Mike's shirt and lifted. His arms went up automatically to allow her to remove it. Her fingers slipped inside the stretchy waistband of his shorts and he caught them, stopped them. He couldn't do this, not if she didn't mean it.

"Sherry, you don't have to—"

She kissed him, stopping his words effectively, her breasts brushing against his naked chest. His hands tightened on hers.

"Hush." Her lips whispered their way across his cheek to his ear. She rose on tiptoe to reach it, leaning into him. "I know I don't have to do anything I don't want to, Mike. So what do you think that means?"

With his hands still gripping hers, she put her arms

around him, pressing her sweet body against his until he trembled with the force of what she did to him. What did she mean? He had trouble finding his brain's logic function. She had to mean that she wanted this, wanted whatever happened.

She set his hands in the small of his back and left them there. Her hands dove back under the waistband of his shorts and she went to one knee as she lowered his remaining clothing to the floor.

But once he'd stepped out, she didn't stand again. She laid her head against his stomach and put her arms around him. He shuddered. Surely she wouldn't—didn't intend—

Her lips closed over his sensitive tip, her tongue touched him, and he cried out. He dropped to his knees with her, wrapping her up in his kiss as he bore her down to the floor again. Sherry rolled, taking them over until he lay on his back with her sprawled on top of him, the open paint can dangerously close to his head. Didn't matter. He was washable.

He tried to follow when she pulled away, but she grabbed his head between her hands and held him still.

"Shh. Slow down," she said, her voice a caress in itself. "Today, I'm in charge. I am going to take care of you."

"Oh—" Mike bit off the oath with a groan. "You're going to kill me."

Her smile was pure wickedness. "Let's see if I really can."

She took his hands and placed them together over his head before she started her experiment. He laced his fingers together and held on tight when she tipped his head up and kissed the pulse just under his chin. The one he felt throbbing clear through his brain. Then she kissed her way down his neck to nip at his collarbone before continuing downward. Her fingers ruffled the light dusting of hair in the center of his chest and her kiss there made him shudder.

His hands came up off the floor to cradle her head, to nudge her lower, and she stopped.

One at a time she caught his wrists, put his hands back over his head and pressed them against the floor. "Leave them."

Mike didn't think he could force words through his throat, so he just nodded. He lost his ability to breathe, as well, when Sherry looked down his body. His buttocks tightened, lifting his hips just a little, inviting her to look more. To touch.

Her hands slid down his stomach and veered off across his hip as she touched her tongue to his nipple. He never realized his hands had moved until she was pressing them back on the floor. At least this time she didn't stop kissing him. Just not where he wanted it most.

He couldn't stop touching her, couldn't leave his hands where she put them. Her wicked exploration had him gasping, moaning and touching whatever he could reach. And still she wouldn't touch him where he most wanted it. Was this erotic torment payback for what he'd done to her last time? The first time they'd made love?

Who cared? He didn't. Not anymore. She was going to kill him if she kept this up another minute.

His control snapped. He grabbed her and flipped her beneath him, knocking the paint can with an elbow. It rocked, but didn't topple. He didn't care. He needed to be inside her. Now.

He had the presence of mind—barely—to find his wallet and the protection he'd started carrying since the party. Then he came back over her and thrust home. Sherry cried out, in passion he was sure, since she wrapped her legs around his back and lifted to meet him as he began to move.

She's mine. Only mine. The words repeated in his brain in rhythm with his pounding motion. His passion rose, consumed him, burst into brilliance at the moment Sherry throbbed around him, and through it all, the thought remained:

He couldn't let her go.

He didn't know how—or even if—he could convince her to stay, but he had to try. Maybe he would still fail, but if he gave up without making any effort, he was a bigger coward than his mother called him.

"Oh. My." Sherry gasped beneath him and Mike immediately shifted his weight onto his elbows.

"You okay?"

"Am I still alive?"

He grinned. "We both seem to have survived your little experiment."

She took a deep breath, lifting her breasts into firmer contact with his chest. "Good. Because it didn't end right."

"No?" Mike pushed her hair back, noticing more paint there than before. Oops. "Seemed to end pretty right to me."

"Well, yes, *that* right was…very right." She poked him in the collarbone. "But I was supposed to be on top."

"Okay, okay. Next time you can be on top."

Sherry paused, looked up at him uncertainly. "Next time?"

"You have to get the experiment right, don't you?" He smiled, hoping to get one back, and did.

"Try try again?" She raised an eyebrow.

"And then practice till it's perfect."

She laughed, hugging him tight. "Sounds like a plan to me."

"You have paint in your hair," he said a long moment later as he rolled away from her.

"What else is new?" She tossed him his underwear.

"More paint."

"Yeah? Well, you have paint on your—" She patted his

backside and Mike twisted to see a fresh handprint, obviously just put there. Damn, he loved this woman.

The thought gave him pause. He loved her. It stopped him cold, but it didn't come as any surprise. It had been building since the day he married her.

The knowledge dug twice as deep into his heart, soared twice as close to the stars as anything he'd felt before. Could he keep her?

Sherry cared about him. He knew that now, but did she care enough? She'd run away from Greeley's money. She claimed to want her own only for the protection it would provide her. Could she mean it?

"We'd better get the rest of this paint on the walls," he said, changing the cover on the paint roller for a fresh, fuzzy one. He handed it to her.

"I can do this part?" She beamed up at him.

"Have at it." He hoped she wouldn't be so enthusiastic he had to go buy more paint. But if it made her happy...

Who would have thought? How many Palm Beach babes got excited over painting? At least one. This one.

Mike dipped the small brush in the can and started on the porch door. Something Tug had said at the party had been coming back to bother him in the weeks since, and it came back again now—that he'd get nothing if he stayed married to Sherry. Did that mean Tug had tied the trust up some way so Mike couldn't touch it, or did it mean something else?

He didn't care for himself, he had enough money to retire tomorrow and never be able to spend it all. But it might matter to Sherry. Maybe that should be the first step in his new, revised campaign—the one to convince her to stay. He should know what Tug meant and how it would affect Sherry.

Eleven

Mike pulled his car into a parking space and turned off the engine, then sat there, gripping the steering wheel tightly enough to keep his hands from shaking. He should have known, should have expected what he just discovered, but after the last week and a half, he'd dropped his defenses.

No typical, money-grubbing, trust-fund baby would get so excited about a few gallons of paint. That's what he'd thought when Sherry bubbled over about painting his kitchen barn red, and his bedroom midnight blue. He'd just laughed and let her go, even if it made his bedroom feel a little like a cave. He didn't mind the dark intimacy when Sherry came so willingly to his bed every night, when she opened her arms and welcomed him in with sweet kisses and soft words, inviting him to lose himself in her warmth.

But it was all an act.

Good thing he'd found out before he was sucked in any

farther. It was bad enough now, when he was just starting to fall in love with her. How far would she have carried the charade? As far as having a child? Mike shuddered. He let go of the steering wheel to open the door and get out of the car. His hands still shook. He balled them into tight fists and hid them in his pockets as he kicked the car door shut. He had to regain control before he went upstairs to confront her.

She would be there. Monday was her day off and his mother would be asleep this time of the afternoon. Even with the nurse, Sherry spent most of her time next door with Clara. Mike took a deep breath, fighting to make it smooth and even. The deep sense of betrayal threatened to rip him apart. He'd never felt anything like it, not even when Blair left him.

Mike touched his jacket, feeling the crinkle of the paper tucked in his inside pocket. He had his proof, a little crumpled, but he'd straightened it out again and folded it carefully away. He took another deep breath, this one smoother than the last, and headed for the elevator.

He found Sherry in the guest bedroom, the one she'd used that first night, sticking paint samples to the wall. She smiled when she saw him, the way she always did, and the sunshine brightness of the lie sliced through him like a blade. He refused to react, keeping his face impassive with some effort. Gradually her smile faded.

"Is something wrong?" She scrambled to her feet. "Clara…?"

"Mom's fine. I checked on her before I came home."

"Then what…?"

How to begin? He'd promised to stay married until her birthday. Just because she'd lied from the first words out of her mouth didn't mean he would break his word. And yet, circumstances weren't what he'd been led to believe. "I think you should move back in with Mom."

Little creases of confusion formed on her forehead. "But...why? Didn't you say she was—"

"She *is* fine. This doesn't have anything to do with Mom. It has to do with you and me."

Her smile returned, hot and smoky. Sherry eased forward, hand out to touch him. Mike flinched away, out of her reach. He didn't dare let her get too close. He was too weak.

"Mike, what's wrong?" Her frown was back. She reached for him again, and again he moved away. "What's happened?"

"Did you think I wouldn't find out?"

"Find out what?" Her confusion sounded so genuine. What an expert liar she was.

"It's all been an act, hasn't it? From the minute you walked into La Jolie. You sat there all day, until you got my attention. Waiting for the boss." He gripped the dresser, wrapping his hands around the edge so he wouldn't be tempted to touch her. "You hooked me on your line and played me like a pro."

"What are you talking about?" Still she pretended innocence.

He swore, unable to take any more, and slammed out of the room. He fled across the living room and yanked open the balcony door, needing the fresh air, the ocean wind on his face.

"Micah?" Sherry had followed him, just as he expected. "I don't understand."

"Don't you?" He spoke without turning, hands braced on the balcony railing, staring out at the waves beyond the beach. "Why did you ask me to marry you?"

"We've been through all that. My father. Greeley—"

"So why haven't I ever seen any sign of the man? Where is he? Who is he?"

"I...I don't know where he's been. He's the heir to some

chemical company that just got bought out by Dupont for a bazillion dollars.''

"If he wanted to marry you so bad, why didn't he ever show up?" And why did the answers matter so much? They shouldn't. Not now that he knew the truth.

"I don't know." Tears choked her voice. He steeled himself against them. "Maybe he didn't want me all that much. Why are you acting like this?"

"Because I don't like getting trapped into marriage with lying, scheming, money-hungry cheats." The words snarled their way out of the knot of pain churning in his gut as finally he looked up at her.

Sherry stared at him, eyes wide, tears streaming down her face. Damn, she was good. "Wh-what?"

"You can stop the act now. I know the truth. Maybe you didn't make this Greeley guy up. I don't know about that. But I do know that you looked around for available millionaires and latched on to the first one you found. Me. Hell, for all I know, you drew my name out of a hat." He couldn't take her looking at him like that, like she was a puppy he'd kicked. She was the one doing all the kicking. She'd stabbed him in the heart. She had no right to look so wounded. Mike retreated into the house.

Of course she followed. "M-millionaire? You're not— you manage a restaurant."

"I *own* the restaurant. I own this building. I've bought and sold more businesses than…than you've bought shoes. I buy them cheap, turn them around, make them profitable, then I sell them for an even bigger profit. Don't pretend you didn't know. Don't pretend that's not why you wanted to marry me."

"But I didn't know." She was crying hard now, sobbing as if her heart would break.

Could he possibly be wrong about her? *No.* He had the proof in his pocket. "Bull. You knew. You gave me a big song and dance about 'just till I get my trust fund,' and all the time you had big plans for me and my money.''

''I didn't.'' She shook her head so her hair flew out straight. ''I don't. I don't care about the money, Mike. I care about you.''

The boom as his hand hit the table echoed around the room. Sherry flinched, crying harder.

''Stop lying to me!'' He tried to shout away the hurt, turn it into anger. ''How do you expect me to believe a word out of your mouth when I know the truth?'' He snatched the paper from his inside pocket and threw it at her.

It caught the air and floated gently to the floor, instead of arrowing hard and fast at her the way he wanted—the way the knowledge had hit him.

Sherry bent to pick it up, swiping her cheeks with the backs of her hands as she opened it. ''What is this?''

''It's a statement.''

''Of what?'' She turned it this way and that, as if that might make its contents more decipherable, as if she didn't already know what it said. More lies.

''Of your trust fund.'' Mike strode across the room again, closing the balcony door enough that the curtains didn't blow halfway to the ceiling. ''The one you're just waiting until your birthday to claim. The one you lied about.''

''I don't understand. Where's the balance?''

Mike stalked toward her and stabbed his finger at the tell-tale numbers. ''Right there. The row of zeros.''

She went pasty white as the blood drained from her face. Her knees collapsed and she crumpled onto the sofa. He might have been alarmed if he didn't already know what a spectacular actress she was.

''It's gone?'' she whispered. ''All of it?''

''Every penny. But then you knew that. I met with the

trust officer after lunch today. Once I proved we were legally married, he was only too happy to show me your assets. Problem is, you don't have any. You and your father cleaned it out eight months ago, remember?''

''There's nothing left...'' Her voice trailed away into silence.

She sat there motionless for so long, staring at the statement, Mike almost began to worry. Almost. But she had to know. How could she not know?

''I...'' Sherry looked up at him then, so innocent, so hurt and bewildered and vulnerable that Mike wanted to hold her.

He wanted to believe her lies, stick his head in the sand and ignore the truth. But if he did, it would only hurt worse when the end finally came. Now, she just ripped loose a vein or two. If he let himself fall any deeper in love, she would rip out his heart and feed it to the vultures.

Sherry stood on wobbly legs. ''I've never lied to you, Micah Scott. I didn't know about any of this.'' She waved the paper at him and their surroundings, at the building he owned. ''I'm the one who's been lied to. By my father, and by you.''

She drew a shaky breath, her chin quivering, and when she spoke, he heard the tears she fought. ''I guess my big mistake was falling in love with you. You, Micah. Not this money I didn't know you had. My mistake. My problem. I'll get over it.''

A pang of conscience struck him as she walked shakily toward the front door. He fought it back—she was a liar, a manipulator—and he lost. ''Where are you going? Home to your parents?''

Sherry paused. ''No, not there. Never there. I'll figure something out.''

''Go to Mom's. Stay there till you know what you want to do.'' Why was he saying this? He needed a clean break.

But he couldn't do it. "I'll send Bruno by with what the club owes you— I'm assuming you don't want to keep working there."

She nodded, forehead against the door. After a long minute, she looked over her shoulder at him. "I've never lied to you, Micah. Not ever." And she was gone.

Sherry stood in the hallway, her hand resting on the handle of the door she'd closed on her hopes for happiness. Her brain felt numb, while her thoughts reeled from one lightning strike to the next. The money was gone. Every penny.

Her mother had left her the trust fund. Nothing else. Not even a string of pearls. Sherry never knew what had happened to all her things. No one had bothered to answer her questions. And now the only sign she'd ever had to know her mother cared about her, at least a little, had vanished. It had been stripped away by a man who cared more about his own comfort than about his daughter's future.

But she wasn't that lost little girl anymore. She didn't need the money. She could survive without it. She wasn't so sure she could survive without her heart.

She tried to swallow back the fresh tears burning down her cheeks and only succeeded in choking on the boulder that had invaded her throat. When had she fallen in love with Mike? It had sneaked up on her bit by bit with each kindness, each smile, each kiss. She suspected she'd fallen a little in love with him that very first night on the beach when he'd been so insistent about looking after her. Nobody had ever done that before.

And he believed she'd set it all up just to get her hands on his money. She should have known he was more than a mere manager. He might have been able to make a deal for rent by managing a building he didn't own, but he'd never have furnished it the way he had. She'd seen the clues but ignored them. She'd wanted to believe Mike was who and what he said he was. But it was all lies.

So what else was new? Sherry took a deep breath and wiped her eyes with the hem of her T-shirt. She'd been lied to before. She would be lied to again. Get over it.

She'd made herself a promise on the moon and the sea that she would stand on her own. She loved Mike, but she could live without him. Obviously, since he hated her, she'd better start getting used to it. The pain wouldn't kill her. It would just feel that way for a while.

Swiping at her eyes once more and hoping she didn't look too horrible, Sherry made herself walk down the hall to Clara's door and knocked. Then she let herself in, calling out quietly to the nurse in case Clara was still asleep. "It's me."

"It's my heart that's broke, not my ears," Clara called from the bedroom. "Come in here and talk to me before I go berserk from boredom and start grabbing for butcher knives."

The duty nurse looked at Sherry across the kitchen island and grinned. "She's in a mood today. Feeling pretty good, so she's got to take it out on everybody around."

Sherry smiled back as best she could and headed to Clara's big sunny bedroom.

The older woman was sitting up in a cushy recliner big enough to swallow her, putting the TV remote through its paces. "How can there be so many channels and nothing on worth watching?" she grumbled, turning her cheek up for a kiss without ever quite looking away from her task.

"I don't know." Sherry fought to keep her voice even and failed miserably, as evidenced by the way Clara's head whipped around.

"What's wrong, sugar?" Clara gripped Sherry's hand tight as she searched her face. "What happened? Is Micah all right?"

"He…he's fine. Can I stay here tonight?"

"No, you may not."

"Wh-what?" Shock started the stupid tears up again. Sherry tried to wipe them away before they showed.

"No. You can't stay here tonight. I don't know what you and that hardheaded son of mine fought about, but whatever it is, you can just march right back over there and straighten it out."

"I tried—"

"Baloney. If you really tried, you'd be over there, not over here." Clara waved her hand at the door. "Now go on. Get."

Now what would she do? Something. She'd think of something. She was a grown woman. Strong. Invincible. Pathetic. Okay, so she wasn't up to roaring just now, but she could by gosh squeak. "Can I at least wash my face before you kick me out?"

Clara sighed. "Oh, all right. I suppose. But hurry up."

Sherry went into the attached bath thinking frantically. She had her car. She could go get her things as soon as Mike left for the club, then wait in the lobby for Bruno to bring her paycheck. She'd earned it. She needed it. But she wouldn't take one thing she hadn't bought with her own money. She splashed the cool water over her burning face one more time and turned off the faucet.

"Are you still here?" Clara called.

"Just leaving." Sherry came to hug Clara, ignoring her attempts to push her away. "I love you, you ornery old woman."

"Humph." Clara shoved harder and Sherry backed up. "You should be saying that to my son. Your husband, re-member?"

"He's an ornery old woman?" Sherry shook her head. "I did. It didn't seem to matter. You take care of yourself, hear me? Mind your nurse."

Clara's eyes narrowed. "Something's not right here. What's going—?"

Sherry fled before Clara could get into her inquisition, and kept going, ignoring the demands that she come back right this instant and explain what in hell was going on.

"Better get back there," she told the nurse as she sailed past, "before she gets any more worked up."

The next day Mike delayed his visit to his mother until after lunch, hoping that Sherry might have gone out. He couldn't take seeing her again so soon. Mom was her usual feisty self, though since her "fainting spell" as she called it, she seemed more spirit than flesh. He talked about the club, danced around the pacemaker subject again, listened to the news relayed from the sister who'd come by that morning and finally gave up the fight with himself.

"Did Sherry go out?" He tried to sound casual, as if the answer didn't matter. Because it didn't.

"Well, how should I know?" Mom picked through the bowl of hard candies on the table beside her chair, hunting the flavor she wanted.

"She stayed here last night." Mike frowned. "Didn't she?"

"No, she did not. I told her to go home to her husband and work things out." She plucked out a pale-yellow candy and pulled at the cellophane wrapper before stopping to stare at him. "Do you mean to tell me she didn't?"

"I guess that's what I'm saying. I haven't seen her." He ran a hand back through his hair, telling himself he didn't have reason to worry. Women like her always landed on their feet.

"What in the world have you done, Micah Thomas Scott?"

"Me?" He threw himself from the chair. "I haven't done anything but find out the truth. That she's a liar and a fraud. She's flat broke, Mom. That trust fund she's so proud of is empty, has been for months. She came after me for my money."

"Did she?"

He could feel his mother's eyes boring holes into his back. He wasn't about to turn around and let her bore them through his eyes into his brain.

"Did she really, Micah?" Mom's voice was gentle. "Do you honestly think that, deep down inside you?"

"Yes." He bit out the word.

"Then why do you care where she is?"

Because I was stupid enough to believe she was different. I was stupid enough to fall in love with her. But he wouldn't say that aloud. "I don't."

The next few weeks proved that statement a lie. Mike quizzed Bruno about delivering her paycheck. She'd met him in the lobby of the building and waited at the elevator as if going back up when he left, according to the bartender's story. She didn't seem upset at the time. She smiled and thanked him for taking the trouble, but she did look as if she might have been crying earlier.

Her car was gone from the garage. All her things were gone from the apartment. Nothing else. She'd left the wedding ring in an envelope with his name on it on the kitchen bar. Everything was as it had been before. As if she had never set foot in his apartment, in his life.

Except that somehow she permeated the air he walked through. Her scent lingered no matter how wide he opened the balcony doors, no matter how hard he let the wind blow through. Even the night it rained, soaking his bed, it wasn't enough to wash her out of his mind.

He missed her. He hated her. He loved her. He wished she had never set foot in his club. And he wished she would walk through the door and never leave again.

A thousand times a day, he shoved memories into a mental vault and spun the wheel to lock them away—her smile, the soft silk of her skin, the music of her laughter. And a thousand and ten times a day, the memories seeped through the cracks back into his brain. Mike didn't bother fighting them at night. He was helpless against the dreams.

By the end of the month, he was getting better. His chest didn't burn all the time. Now and again he slept through the night without dreaming of her. Then he got the letter.

Addressed to him at the club in a handwriting he didn't recognize, the cheap discount store envelope bore no return address. Curious, Mike slit it open. The sheaf of papers inside confused him for a moment, because they came with a check attached, made out to him for three hundred dollars. Then he saw Sherry's signature at the bottom.

His heart sped up before his brain caught on. She'd signed it *Sherry Scott*. She was still using his name. Three hundred dollars was the amount of the extra money he'd put in her last paycheck to tide her over until she got back on her feet. Why? Was she refusing to take money from him on principle? Or did she just want him to think so?

He was going to make himself crazy wondering. Mike tossed the check aside, not watching where it fell, and looked through the papers. He wasn't hunting for a note from her, just…something. It took another moment to realize what he held. She'd sent him divorce papers.

Not nice, neat, lawyer-generated documents, but fill-in-the-blank forms copied out of some how-to-be-your-own-lawyer book. He could see a faint library stamp at the bottom of one page. Sherry had carefully filled in all the blanks, printing "NONE" in large block letters in the spousal support box. And she had signed her name.

Mike grabbed up a pen and froze with it poised over the line marked with the X. His hand didn't want to move. He forced the pen down, pressed the point into the paper, but he couldn't make himself sign.

The papers might not be legal. He should just call his own lawyer, have him draw up something airtight. He should have done it already. He didn't know why he hadn't.

Because you're still in love with her, you idiot.

He threw the pen across the room, then he shoved all the papers off the desk. It wasn't enough. Anger still raged through him. He gripped the edge of his desk, fighting the urge to upend it. Destroying his furniture wouldn't help anything. He had to get up, had to move.

Mike paced, trying to shake off the mood. How could he still love her after everything she'd done? How could mere paper make him want to tear at everything around him until it was as destroyed as he was? How could it still hurt like this?

Stupid, but he felt that if he signed his name to that paper, something precious would die. People talked about how divorce was a death of sorts—the death of a marriage. That wasn't the case here. Their marriage had never been alive in the first place. It was a paper construct, built on lies.

But it hadn't felt like paper. Not while he was in it. It felt like…happiness. Bone-deep. Could that exist on a foundation of lies? Mike stacked his fists, one on top of the other, against the wall and leaned his forehead on them, trying to clear away the anger enough to think.

Even when he'd been so besotted with Blair, his happiness had been a thin curtain over a sense of unease. Her defection had hurt but it hadn't surprised him. Sherry's betrayal had come out of nowhere, blindsiding him so he hadn't been able to even drive. He'd been through this before, seen the greed and speculation in women's eyes. He knew what it looked like, could spot it at a hundred paces.

Had he ever seen it in Sherry's? Could he have been wrong?

Mike struggled to banish the emotions clouding his memory. He had been so hurt, using his anger as a shield to prevent any more of it. Had he missed seeing the truth? He pressed his fingers against his eyes, pushing aside visions of Sherry in his bed, Sherry laughing at him across the table, and tried to summon up that last day. That last time he saw her.

She'd gone so white. Almost fallen. Could she truly have not known the money was gone?

No one less than the best actress in the world could have faked that reaction. Was Sherry that good? He wouldn't have thought so, but…

Either it was all lies from the beginning or none of it was.

And if none of it was… Dear sweet heaven, what had he done?

Sherry ducked inside the kitchen door and leaned against the wall. Her shift had ended, but she was too tired to head out without taking a little breather first. She had a long walk back to her room, and her feet were already killing her. But she would make it. She'd made it this far, hadn't she?

Two months without Mike. Her waitress job here at an Orlando resort, even with all the hours on her feet, the cranky customers and crying children, was a snap compared to living without Mike. But she hadn't cried in her sleep for a whole week now. She hardly ever imagined she saw him striding with his long easy gait through the resort lobby.

She'd filled out the divorce papers and mailed them. All he had to do was sign them and file them with the court there in Palm Beach. The final steps wouldn't require more than a little time. Surely it would be over soon.

With a sigh Sherry pushed off the wall and untied her pocketed apron. She carefully removed her tips and tucked them away before hanging the apron on the hook marked with her name on masking tape. The tips made the difference between bare subsistence and almost making a living. She didn't dare drop a penny. She slipped out the back with a wave at the boss and started the long walk through the resort grounds to the dorm-like rooms where the employees who lived on-site were housed.

A lean masculine shape caught her peripheral vision, haunting her with its familiarity. She ignored it. Mike wasn't here. Wouldn't be, even if he knew where she was, which he didn't. He'd lied to her, pretending to be something he wasn't, then he'd accused her of doing what he'd done. He jumped to conclusions, made faulty assumptions and refused to listen to reason. She didn't want anything to do with a man like that.

Which was another big fat lie. She loved him, and she was terribly afraid she always would.

He'd never actually told her about this woman who'd broken his heart, but Sherry could put the hints and clues together. She'd seen how men with money were pursued, not just in Palm Beach but everywhere she'd traveled. She couldn't really blame him for his conclusions and assumptions. She couldn't even blame him for refusing to listen. It was natural to throw defenses up high to prevent any more hurt. She'd done it herself enough times. And if he didn't want her, then that was that.

"Do you have any idea of the hell you've put me through?"

Mike's deep voice sent Sherry spinning around. He stood on the walk behind her. That single lock of rich brown hair spilled over his forehead drawing attention to his eyes, thundercloud gray in the bright summer afternoon. The tiny lines and bruised look around them spoke of strain. He stood there in his open-necked shirt and casual slacks seeming at first glance relaxed and coolly collected, but Sherry could see the intensity hovering beneath the surface. He fairly quivered with it.

And even knowing what he thought of her, she wanted to take him in her arms and soothe the strain away.

"Say something." He took a step closer, still too far away to touch.

"What do you want me to say?"

"I don't know. Hello, Mike. Goodbye, Mike. Go to hell, Mike. Something." Another step. His gaze held her helpless.

Her lips curved into a momentary smile. "Hello, Mike."

He took one more step and reached up to brush her hair behind her ear, freezing for half an instant before he touched her, then following through with his intention. "You look good."

She allowed another half smile, holding herself rigid to keep from leaning into his brief touch. She wouldn't be so needy. "Thank you."

Mike looked around at the manicured lawns, the lush flowers. "What are you doing here?"

"Working."

He closed his eyes a second before opening them again and settling into his "business face." "Do you have a few minutes? Or are you heading to work? Could we meet later, for dinner maybe? We have things to discuss."

Sherry swallowed down the hurt. It took her two tries, but she did it. At least well enough to sound reasonably cool when she spoke. "Is this about the divorce papers?"

Color flooded his face and receded again. He opened his mouth to speak, closed it, then started over. "Yes."

"You could have filed them there in Palm Beach County. You didn't have to come track me down." She stared out over the tennis courts, unable to look at him.

"Yes." He stepped in front of her, making her look. "I did. And it wasn't easy. It's taken me weeks to find you. When I learned you'd sold your car—I thought I'd lost you."

"No big loss." She couldn't take much more of this. "Since you'd already kicked me out. No big deal."

"It's a very big deal. More than you can imagine." Again he brushed back her windblown hair. "Have dinner with me."

She didn't dare. Already it was too hard to keep from throwing herself at him and begging him to forgive her, though she'd done nothing requiring forgiveness. "I don't think so." But she didn't want him to think she was afraid of him. Even if she was. She feared what he made her feel. "I'm just coming off work. I'm too tired to want to go out again. Now is fine."

He nodded. "All right." He surveyed their surroundings again, then took her elbow, his grasp almost a caress. "There's a bench under that tree."

"Why not do it right here?" Sherry balked. She didn't want to spend any more time with him than she had to. Seeing him again made her feel like a drunk falling off the sobriety wagon. One taste and she would be completely lost.

"Humor me." He drew her along. "It's hot. There's shade under the tree."

When they reached it, Sherry plopped gracelessly down on the bench. To her supreme relief, Mike remained standing. He ran his hands back through his hair the way he did when he didn't know what to do. Usually Clara prompted the finger combing.

"How is your mother?" Sherry asked. "Did you talk her into getting the pacemaker?"

He nodded, his mind obviously elsewhere. "She's having it done next week. She'd want you to be there."

"Maybe I'll come." Just because Mike hated her was
no reason to give up the friendship with his mother. She
was grateful Clara didn't hate her, too. She needed to get
this torture over with. "Do you have a pen?"

"What?" He blinked at her, then seemed to comprehend
the question. "Oh. Sure." He pulled one from his shirt
pocket and handed it to her.

"Where are the papers?"

"What papers?"

"The divorce papers. The ones you want me to sign."

"I tore them up."

Why did he have to do this to her? "I already signed
those. I'm assuming you tracked me down because you had
your lawyer draw up a new set." She'd managed to figure
that out, understand his reason for being here, despite the
way he turned her brain into pure carbonation. "A more
airtight set. Make sure I don't get any of your precious
money."

"I don't care about the money. I never did."

She believed him, but some vengeful spark flared up
wanting payback. "Right. That's why you kicked me out
the minute you learned I didn't have any."

His head jerked up, the pain in his eyes making Sherry
instantly wish she could call the words back. His pain slid
into sorrow so deep her eyes burned with sympathetic tears.

"I deserve that, I suppose." Mike sank onto the far end
of the bench, dropping his head in his hands. "Damn, what
a mess."

Sherry clung tight to the cast-iron armrest to hold herself
in place. Otherwise, she'd be pressed to Mike's side telling
him everything would be okay. It wouldn't. At least, she
didn't think so. "Micah, why are you here? You said it was
about the divorce…?"

"I tore up the papers." He sat up straight, staring across
the flowers at the tennis court.

"You said that already. So where are the new ones?"

"There aren't any."

"There…? Why not?"

Mike looked at her then. His ravaged expression tore at the protective scar tissue around her heart, and the faint light of hope in his eyes had it beating faster. "I don't want a divorce. Come home with me, Sherry. Be my wife." His throat moved as he swallowed down some emotion he didn't want her to see. "I can't stand seeing you like this."

Ah. Now she understood. Guilt had reared its ugly head once more. That overgrown sense of responsibility of his had him tightly in its grip.

She smiled. "I'm doing just fine, Micah. Maybe it's not what I grew up with, but I have everything I need. They're moving me into management training next week. I really can take care of myself." She laid her hand gently over his where it rested beside him on the bench. "I don't need you to rescue me."

"Hell, I know that. That's not why I'm here." He turned his hand over and gripped hers with crushing strength. "Rescue me, Sherry. Rescue *me*."

She could only stare as he slid off the bench onto his knees in the grass and pressed a kiss to the back of her hand. "Mike, what…? Get up from there."

"I can't. This is what you've done to me. This is where you've put me. I'm in hell without you." He kept his head bent, lips against her fingers, teasing them with his breath as he spoke. "You said you loved me. Was that the truth?"

Hot tears blurred her vision, finally spilling over. She was almost afraid to speak, almost afraid to hope. But this was the new Sherry, the woman he had helped her become, and this woman didn't back down from her fears. She took his face between her hands and tipped it up until she could see his beautiful gray eyes.

"I've never lied to you, Micah," she said. "Ever."

"I lied to you." He rested his hands on her knees, lightly, carefully, as if afraid she might knock them off. "I'm sorry. I was—"

She shook her head, pressing her thumbs across his lips to silence him. "I understand. It's all right. As long as you don't do it again."

"Never." He took oath.

"Do you really want to stay married to me?" She bit her lip, the old uncertainties battering her new confidence.

"God, yes." He leaned forward, apparently intending to rest his head on her knees along with his hands.

"Why?" She needed the words.

Mike's head jerked up, and he stared at her. Then understanding came into his eyes and his smile warmed them. "We both already know I'm an idiot. I just proved it again."

He took her hands in his and raised them one at a time to his lips for a tender kiss. "Sherry Eloise Nyland Scott, I love you with all of my heart. Will you please do me the honor of being my wife?" He reached into his pants pocket and drew out the wedding ring she'd left lying on the bar. Clara's ring.

"I want more than paper," he said. "I want promises. Commitment. The till-death-do-us-part kind. Kids. The whole package. From you, Sherry. Only from you. Because I love you."

"Really?" She wanted so much to believe it. "Truly?"

"Hell, woman, what more do you want? You've already got me on my knees." He pushed the ring onto her finger. "Why do you think I went so crazy? Because I was so crazy in love with you that I couldn't stand to think you didn't love me back. And I didn't dare believe you did. But you do. Now, are you coming home with me, or do I have to throw you over my shoulder and carry you there? Because that's your only choice here. You love me and I love you and we're married and that's all there is to it.''

Laughing through the tears streaming down her cheeks, Sherry launched herself at Mike, knocking him flat on the grass, covering his face with kisses. Her assault caught him off guard, but he recovered in seconds, rolling to lie over her and capture her lips in a long, sweet, hot, wet kiss.

''Thank heaven,'' he murmured when he paused to catch his breath. ''For a minute there, I was worried.''

''For a minute there, so was I.'' Sherry snuggled in. ''Then you told me what was what. You only talk like that to people you really love.''

''Don't you ever forget it.'' Mike lowered his head for another kiss.

The loud clearing of a throat interrupted him. A balding man in a resort management uniform stood scowling down at them. Sherry didn't recognize him, but that didn't mean anything. The resort had a lot of management. ''Fraternization between employees and guests is strictly forbidden,'' he said.

Mike stood and lifted Sherry to her feet. ''Good thing I'm not a guest, then, because I have every intention of fraternizing her brains out.''

''Doesn't matter,'' Sherry said airily. ''I'm not an employee anymore, either.'' She pulled her ID badge from her pocket and dropped it in the man's hand. ''I'll turn in my key up front as soon as I'm packed.''

''B-but you can't just quit. It's high season.''

''Sorry.'' She took Mike's hand and tugged him down the path after her.

''But why? Where are you going?''

She looked up into Mike's face, seeing what she'd been hunting all her life. ''I'm going home. With my husband. Where I belong.''

*　　*　　*　　*　　*

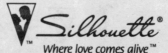

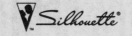

ERICA SPINDLER

D E A D   R U N

*USA TODAY bestselling author Erica Spindler proves
once again that she is a master at delivering
chilling shockers that explore the sometimes
twisted nature of the human psyche.*

When Rachel Ames disappears after leaving a strange message on
her sister's answering machine, Liz Ames heads to Key West to find
out what's happened. Within days of her arrival, the area is plagued
by a mysterious suicide, another disappearance and the brutal murder
of a teenage girl. But no one believes these events are linked to
Rachel's disappearance.

Only Rick Wells, a former cop, is willling to listen to Liz. And as they
get closer to the truth, they begin to uncover an unspeakable evil from
which they may not escape unscathed.

"...savvy amounts of sex and moral outrage, investigagtion and con-
frontation, psychology and romance." —*Publishers Weekly*

On sale in May 2003 wherever paperbacks are sold!

MES683